W9-BVH-909

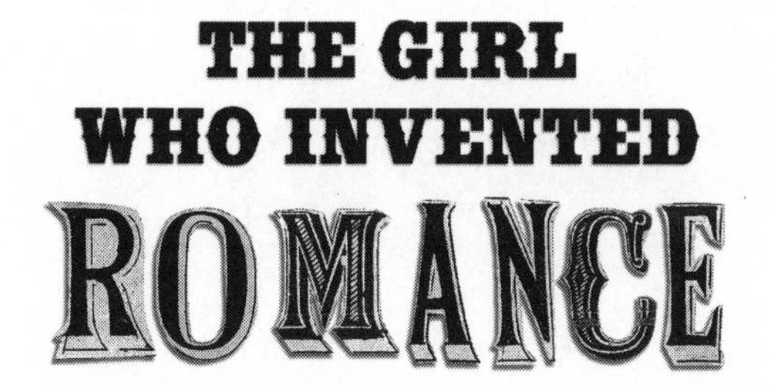
THE GIRL
WHO INVENTED
ROMANCE

Also by **CAROLINE B. COONEY**

The Janie Books:

The Face on the Milk Carton

Whatever Happened to Janie?

The Voice on the Radio

What Janie Found

The Time Travel Quartet:

Both Sides of Time

Out of Time

For All Time

Prisoner of Time

Other Books:

Family Reunion

Goddess of Yesterday

The Ransom of Mercy Carter

Tune In Anytime

Burning Up

What Child Is This?

Driver's Ed

Twenty Pageants Later

Among Friends

CAROLINE B. COONEY

DELACORTE PRESS

Published by
Delacorte Press
an imprint of
Random House Children's Books
a division of Random House, Inc.
New York

Copyright © 1988 by Caroline B. Cooney
Jacket illustration copyright © 2005 by Jackie Parsons

Originally published by Bantam Books in 1988

All rights reserved. No part of this book may be reproduced or transmitted in any form or by any means, electronic or mechanical, including photocopying, recording, or by any information storage and retrieval system, without the written permission of the publisher, except where permitted by law.

The trademark Delacorte Press is registered in the U.S. Patent and Trademark Office and in other countries.

Visit us on the Web! www.randomhouse.com/teens
Educators and librarians, for a variety of teaching tools, visit us at
www.randomhouse.com/teachers

Library of Congress Cataloging-in-Publication Data

Cooney, Caroline B.
The girl who invented romance.
Summary: While waiting for her first big romance and observing the sometimes rocky love affairs of her parents and brother, sixteen-year-old Kelly develops a board game called Romance.
ISBN: 0-385-73239-2 (tr. pbk.)
ISBN: 0-385-90259-X (GLB)
[1. Love—Fiction.] I. Title.
PZ7.C7834Gi 1988 [Fic] 87-37436

The text of this book is set in 11.5-point Goudy.

Book design by Marci Senders

Printed in the United States of America

First Delacorte Press Edition May 2005

10 9 8 7 6 5 4 3 2

For Beverly, who made the game better
and for Sayre, who named them Flops and Swaps
and with thanks to Phill Marth, art teacher
at Westbrook High School

CHAPTER

I was filling out a magazine quiz to see if my marriage was stable.

"You're sixteen, Kelly," said my best friend. "You don't have a boyfriend, let alone an unstable marriage."

"That just makes it more challenging. I have to dream up a husband, work my way through five years of marriage, and analyze our relationship."

We sprawled on the blue denim bedspread in my room while I finished the quiz. "I got a seventy-three, Faith," I told her.

"What does seventy-three mean?"

I flipped pages. "It means my husband and I are not yet verging on divorce, but we should be aware that we have serious marital difficulties that are going to pose major problems if we don't face them right now."

I dropped the magazine on the floor and lowered my face right into the bedspread. I've been trying to destroy this denim since the day I bought it, so I can have something fragile and pretty instead. But nothing can damage a denim coverlet. Not dirty shoes, spilled perfume, pizza topping or aerobic exercises.

"It makes me sad," said Faith. "You haven't even met this guy yet, and already your marriage is in trouble."

The magazine had fallen open to a home-decorating page. Here was a bedroom for dreams: open and airy, in soft pale colors, no junk around (like my hair dryer, books, makeup, souvenirs, sweaters that don't fit, sweaters that do fit, homework, new laptop). The magazine model was also soft and pale, but you knew that lined up outside her door were dozens of men yearning for her. She just had that confident look.

"That confident look," said Faith, "is because she's getting paid so much. She probably doesn't have a date tonight either, Kelly."

"We should have gone to the basketball game," I said. "Then at least we'd be having fun."

"We were at basketball games Tuesday and Thursday," she said. "How many times a week can a girl watch Will, Scott, Mario, Angie and Jeep?"

I looked at her.

"You're right," she admitted instantly. "A girl could admire those guys every night of the week."

I rolled over. My cheek had a trench line from being pressed against a seam in the denim. If we went to the basketball game now, I'd have to wear a mask. "You know what let's do?" I said, struck by a brilliant idea. "Let's invent a romance game."

"I'm sick of games. I want a real romance."

"Maybe one will come out of this. Three of the five starters on our basketball team are in sociology class with us, right?"

"Right."

"And sociology is a totally boring forty-five-minute stretch of time five days a week. Right?"

"Right."

"So let's turn the classroom into a game room. Let's make up rules and play for boys."

"Oh, Kelly," said Faith, really annoyed with me. "I'm not like Megan or Honey. I can't glance a boy's way and have him get all excited and flirty. What do you mean, 'play for boys'? I've been going in and out of crushes since I was twelve and what do I have to show for it? Not a single date. I've read every romance book there is, and every article in every magazine from *Seventeen* to *Cosmo*, and what do I have junior year? Every weekend free. Don't let's talk about playing for boys. I can't do it, I don't know how, I've given up. Tomorrow I plan to hurl myself down the cellar stairs anyway."

This was Faith's biggest threat. Her house happens to be a ranch built on a slab. But hey, it sounds impressive.

"Who's your crush on this week?" I said. Faith is always in the grip of a crush. The crush seizes her, rules her life and guides her activities. The worst of it is, the boy never notices. I take that back. Once, in ninth grade, the boy noticed. He fled so thoroughly, she never saw him again to keep the crush alive.

"Angie," Faith said dreamily.

That was definitely a dream. Angie—actually Angelo Angelotti—is the beloved star of the Cummington basketball team. All five of our starters are stars, but it's hard to get excited about, say, the stardom of Will, who is very tall, very bony and so conceited I think he may have spoken to six people in the last year, all of whom were teammates or the coach. It's also hard to get excited about the stardom of Scott, who is personality-free and has the IQ of a cold day in January.

That leaves you with Angie, who has such a terrific time playing basketball that you can't keep your eyes off him (you wouldn't keep your eyes off him anyway, because he's so totally cute), and with Jeep—actually George Peters, initials G.P., leads to Jeep—who is centerfold material. Handsome like a soap opera star, with strong memorable features, thick windblown dark hair and soft sad dark eyes.

I forgot Mario.

Everybody forgets Mario. I'm sure nobody ever has a crush on him. He scores almost as often as Will, but while Will is very tall, so you can distinguish him from the other players, Mario is just sort of there. This is probably the last time I'll need to mention Mario.

If Faith had a crush on Angie, she was standing in line with a lot of other girls, and Angie has never been known to date a girl twice.

"There are eleven boys in sociology class," I said to Faith. "There are three basketball stars, right? Will, Jeep and Angie. Right?"

"Right. And two of the other boys are Stephen and Alan, who both have steady girlfriends. And two are Avery and Kenny, who are both extremely total losers. And—"

"Be quiet. I'm planning the game. Don't interrupt."

Faith rolled her eyes. She got off the bed, wandered around my room and landed in front of my fingernail polish collection. Last Christmas my two grandmothers, my aunt and the neighbor I babysit for all gave me enormous gift sets of nail polish. I could go into retail right off my dresser. "Can I try the silver decals and the Roseblush Frost?" said Faith.

"You may have the silver decals and the Roseblush Frost. Here's how our game will go, Faith. I've worked it out in my mind. We'll walk into sociology class on Monday."

"I'm with you. We're walking into sociology."

"And there are eleven boys in the room."

"If you count Chuckie, who in my opinion does not qualify as human, never mind being the right gender."

"I am counting Chuckie. This is a game of chance. You take risks."

"I hate chance. I like skill," said Faith.

"If we had any skill, we'd be off somewhere tonight with the boys of our choice."

"Good point." Faith stroked Roseblush Frost onto her left-hand fingernails with precision. Faith's hands never quiver. Mine do, so my nails have a sticky, confused look. When even your fingernails are confused, you know you're in trouble. "Okay," I said. "We each have to pick a boy and we'll work on him. The selections will be by chance."

Faith shuddered. "If chance gives me Chuckie, or Avery, or Kenny, I'm leaving town."

"Maybe you'll get Angie, though."

Faith started to tell me about how wonderful Angie was, but I knew that as well as she did, so it was a boring conversation. If she went and had a crush on, say, Kenny, who belongs on zoo-cage-cleanup detail, it would be interesting.

Sickening. Humiliating. But interesting.

So I interrupted her. "We'll figure out some kind of countdown that we cannot know until class begins. Then we'll do some sort of Eenie, Meenie, Minie, Mo and find out who each of us plays the game with."

"But what's the game?"

"I haven't figured that out yet. Don't rush me. We creative types need time."

"If we're going to spend that much time," said Faith, who, when it comes to me, does not have as much faith as I would like, "I'll get out the Monopoly game, because we're going to be up till dawn anyway."

Faith and I began playing board games with Candy Land when we were really little, and we've never abandoned the pleasure of board games. They're always waiting for you in those rectangular boxes, full of surprises and satisfactions. You know how when you're in the car, you can talk over anything, whether the driver is your parent or your friend? Cars just help you talk? It's true of board games. They help you talk.

Not that I am usually needy in that area.

Faith finished her right hand and began peeling tiny silver decals and placing them diagonally on her long perfect nails. Faith is very pretty in a sweet, plump way. *Plump* is an exaggeration. She's a little thick in the waist. It's just that I'm so thin, I get carried away by other people's figures. I'm not thin-attractive, calling to mind words like *willowy* or *slender*. I'm thin-scary, so that other people's mothers are always muttering in undertones, "Does she have anorexia?" "No, Mom, Kelly's shaped like a pencil. There's nothing she can do about it." "She could try eating."

"Okay, here's the plan," I told Faith. "We get our boy. Then we have to start down a path, like squares on a Monopoly board, to attract him."

"If it's Angie, I like it. If it's Kenny, pardon me while I gag."

"Just gag over the denim spread, will you? I'm trying to ruin it."

"Nothing will ruin it. You will give it in perfect condition to your grandchildren."

"Now there's a happy thought. It implies that I'm going to get married one day, which means I will surely go out with at least one boy."

"You won't be so happy if you draw Kenny."

I ignored her. "We're going to take dice into class. The first number we roll is the vertical seat row. The second number we roll is the seat within that row. That's the boy we get."

"Except what if you roll a girl?" said Faith.

I had forgotten about girls. There were quite a few in sociology.

"We'll come back to that," said Faith kindly. "Get to the good part. What are the moves?"

I tapped my palm with a pencil. I always think better with a pencil. It's a problem in computer class. I have to hold the thinking pencil in my teeth. "Square one," I said, reflecting on every magazine quiz, self-help article and lovelorn letter I have ever read. Thousands. Possibly millions. And how improved am I? Maybe I should ask for my money back on all those issues. "First move is, you have to smile at him."

"I can handle that," said Faith. "My braces are off and my lip gloss is new."

"Square two. Notice him."

"You said that very intensely, Kelly. In what way are we supposed to *notice* him?"

"Absorb every detail. Be terribly aware. Soak it up."

"Why?"

"Future reference."

"Okay," agreed Faith. "Square two, I'm noticing him. What's square three?"

"Talk to him."

"In public? If I land on Kenny, I'd rather have anthrax."

"Everything has to be in public. That way we develop poise."

"I doubt it," said Faith. "This already sounds like something a ten-year-old would do and we're sixteen."

"You have no faith," I accused her.

Faith just looked at me. She detests her name. She feels that F names are frowsy and frumpy and fat. Whereas Jodie or Laurie or Ally (taking the traditional name route) or Swin or Cherith or Zandra (the nontraditional route)—those are names romance can take and run with.

"Square four," I said, "will be *sit next to him.*"

Now we were at the tricky part.

We do not have assigned seats in sociology or anywhere else except study hall, where there are so many of us, they don't check off by name, but by position on a grid—which leads to a lot of deceit and cover-up—but nevertheless, people tend to sit in the same places every day. Back-row people get tense and anxious if forced to approach the front row, and outer-edge people get very worked up when placed in the middle. People who have to be next to a best friend or die, and people who have to be at a great distance from an enemy or kill—they tolerate no change.

Sociology class is not full. I think there are nineteen or twenty of us. So there are extra desks but the same ones are always empty. If Faith or I suddenly shifted into one, people would get all confused. And if one of us took somebody else's seat, that person would get all irritable. And what would the explanation be? "Oh, I'm just in square four; don't worry about a thing."

"Hmmm," said Faith, regarding seat position.

"You are willing to do anything for Angie, aren't you?" I coaxed.

"Yes, but this is a game of chance. If I get Chuckie or Kenny, the only thing I'm willing to do for them is destroy their photographs so the yearbook editor doesn't know they exist."

It was at this moment that my bedroom door was flung open hard enough for the handle to dent the wall. Megan came in sobbing and my life changed.

Megan did not come in with that purpose in mind. She came in hoping to change *her* life. (Actually she wanted to change her boyfriend Jimmy's life; she wanted him dead, which is as major a change as most of us will ever encounter, but she was *pretending* she wanted to change *her* life.)

"He dumped me," said Megan dramatically, shaking so hard with sobs that her tears spattered on Faith and on me.

"Have a seat," said Faith, patting the bed.

Megan, Faith and I have shared things forever. That's the trouble with living in a development. All our parents bought new houses in Fox Meadow when we were babies. There was never a meadow, let alone foxes, but there were supposed to be hundreds of houses. Something went wrong and they built only a few dozen. I've known every family in Fox Meadow since nursery school. When I was little, I loved this. If your mother didn't have any good snacks around, you could wander through Megan's kitchen or Faith's kitchen. And if Faith's mother wouldn't let her watch a particular television show, there was sure to be room in front of the Smith television, and Mrs. Smith had so many little kids, she never noticed one more or less in front of the tube, and she certainly never cared what they watched.

But now that I am sixteen, I would rather not live in Fox Meadow. I am tired of knowing all about everybody. I am tired of them knowing all about me. Mrs. Smith, for example, saying, "Since you're always free on Saturday nights, Kelly, can I sign you up to babysit for the next two months?" I am especially tired of Megan landing on me whenever she needs company, without even knocking on the front door, never mind my bedroom door.

"He dumped me," she repeated tragically. "I hate that word *dump*. Can't you just see this obscene pile of refuse, thrown down by massive trucks, seagulls circling overhead like small white vultures, and me—lying on top. Dumped."

Megan always has dates.

In fourth grade, when the rest of us hadn't even gotten our braces *on*, never mind *off*, Megan was holding hands with Ricky out on the playground. I remember how we'd say, "Eeeeuh, Megan, yuck! Why do you want to touch a boy?"

So it was hard to be sympathetic about Jimmy. Next weekend, she'd just go out with somebody else. Megan had an inexhaustible supply of boys. I could never figure out where she met them, let alone how she attracted them.

"Dumped for a girl he met when he went bowling," said Megan. "It makes me quite ill. Bowling. It has no status. He could at least dump me for a girl he met skiing. Hand me your tissue box."

I knew then that Faith and I would never mention my silly little romance game, not with Megan and her ten hundred previous dates sitting on the bed with us. I looked down into the open Monopoly game box. There were extra dice there. I might just take one to school and play my silly game by myself.

"You know what I want?" said Megan, sniffing.

Presumably Jimmy.

"I want an affair like your mother's, Kelly."

I was outraged. "My mother is not having an affair."

"The affair she's having with your father, dummy. Every time I come here, he's just bought your mother chocolate or a bouquet of violets or a special card. And how long have they been married? Forever. Longer than any of us have even been alive."

"I should hope so," I said grumpily.

I disliked talking about my parents' romance. It is beautiful and I do love seeing them. They're forty and still setting the standard by which everybody in Fox Meadow goes—notes to each other tucked under the windshield wipers, the special silver charm, the perfect surprise. But it's hard to live in a house that is wall-to-wall romance and not be able to participate one single red rose's worth. My older brother, Parker, literally closes his eyes whenever they get romantic. I used to think it embarrassed him, but now I think he's disgusted by it. Maybe he thinks they're too old and too married.

But then, Parker himself was such a mystery to me right then that who knows?

Because my brother, Parker, was dating Wendy Newcombe. Wendy is the Queen of Romance. Exquisitely pretty, very funny, terribly smart. She writes a daily school soap opera, which we listen to after the principal's announcements. She dates only princes, like Jeep.

Now, Parker is nice. In fact, very nice. When he graduated from middle school, he was voted Nicest Boy and I don't think anybody would change that vote four years later. But what kind of adjective is *nice*? You can't call Parker dramatic or romantic or handsome. He's my brother and I love him—everybody loves him—but Wendy dumped Jeep for my brother Parker and that's amazing.

Jeep has about eight hundred wonderful qualities, from sexy to sweet, from athletic to gorgeous. Park has one wonderful quality. You wonder what Wendy had been thinking of to make that trade. Whatever it was, she was thinking of it constantly.

You should have seen Wendy follow Parker around.

She ran the long way through the corridors between classes just to catch a glimpse of my brother going into chem lab. Once in sociology she actually forgot to take a test, and when Ms. Simms said, "Wendy? You're not taking the test?" Wendy said, "Oh my goodness! Oh dear!" and blushed and added, "I guess I was thinking about Parker."

Parker isn't in our sociology class, but Jeep is. Jeep cringed. He has good features for cringing, although I prefer to imagine his features in terms of kissing and serenading. I can think of no time I would put Parker's features ahead of Jeep's. Even though he's my brother and I'm very loyal. Well, sort of loyal.

Sometimes I think romance is a mystical game. You've been dealt cards you don't know what to do with. You play by rules nobody else seems to be following because they were given a different set of instructions. Or maybe you don't play at all. You can't seem to toss the right combination to start the game.

"Oh well," said Megan, mopping up the last of her tears and throwing Jimmy out with the tissue. "Let's play Monopoly. I'll be banker. Next to boys I like money best." She said, "Oh well," with the reverse inflection. Instead of her voice sinking with despair, it lifted cheerily. Her "Oh well" was looking forward to a new day.

"I'll be the iron," said Faith, choosing her game piece.

"I'll be the Scottie dog," said Megan, choosing hers.

The phone rang.

I keep my phone under the bed because there's so much essential junk on my bedside table. I leaned over backward so that my vertebrae made splintering noises, and I reached down under. My hair, which is absolutely straight and very thin, like my body, fell around me like a silvery gold waterfall and splashed on my carpet. About the only thing I really like about myself is my hair. Yellow silk ribbons.

I groped for the phone and clicked it on. "Hello?"

"Hello, Kelly? It's Wendy. Wendy Newcombe?"

The princess of Cummington High is in two classes with me and has been dating my brother for three months and she thinks I won't recognize her name? "Hi, Wendy," I said. "He isn't home. He's at play practice."

Parker was stage manager of the school production of *The Music Man*. Wendy didn't like this. She wanted Park to take her to the basketball games. Parker didn't like that because he would certainly be compared to Jeep, out there racking up baskets and generally being a top-notch jock.

"Oh," said Wendy sadly. "I thought he'd be home by now."

Wendy's voice is very expressive. I had to bite my lips to keep from offering to run over and stay with her until Park got back. "Shall I give him a message?" I said. "Is something wrong?"

"No," said Wendy, all forlorn, like a little girl who's lost her mother in the crowd. "I just wanted to talk. No subject. Just . . . hear his voice."

Wendy Newcombe, Queen of Romance, so in love with my brother Parker she just had to hear his voice.

What if I never got a phone call from a boy who just had to hear my voice? What if the only tears I ever shed were not from love, but from lack of it?

"What's the matter, Kell?" said Faith. "You stuck under there?" She and Megan yanked me up and I shrieked to cover the sounds of my backbone twisting and to change my face from the despair I felt.

We arranged ourselves cross-legged around the Monopoly board, which we spread in the middle of the bed. We put props under the board so it would lie evenly and the pieces and cards wouldn't slide down onto our toes. I decided to be the top hat and I picked it up, looking down at the familiar squares. Railroads, utilities . . .

"Don't you wish there were boys on these squares?" I said. "You wouldn't buy properties, you'd get boys. You wouldn't win dollars, you'd win dates."

"I don't think there is a board game like that," said Megan.

"But if there were, I would buy it," said Faith. She put the three players at GO.

"I have poster board," I said. "We could copy out the squares but put boys' names where the streets are. Like here." I pointed to the powder blue squares facing me. "We could substitute Angie and Jeep and Will for Connecticut, Vermont and Oriental."

Megan and Faith didn't even bother to listen. Megan took the first turn. Megan always takes the first turn and I am always annoyed and I have never said anything.

I didn't say anything this time, either, except, "I'm sure I have poster board somewhere, but my room is too messy for me to find it. I'll cut computer paper into squares instead."

I taped boy squares over the streets and penciled little cartoons of the basketball starters on them. I wrote their names in what was supposed to be romantic script but was actually just messy handwriting.

"You're going to ruin the board," complained Megan. "When you peel that junk off, you'll tear the whole surface."

"The boys have to have values," I said. "Like property. But not dollars. Let's give every boy a numerical rating. One to ten." I stuck Mario and Scott onto Ventnor Avenue and Marvin Gardens.

"Jeep's a ten," said Megan.

"No," said Faith. "Angie's the ten. There cannot be more than one ten in the game, and it goes to Angie."

"Jeep is more handsome," said Megan.

"Angie is more wonderful." Faith wrote *10* under his sketch.

Megan glared at us both. "You can't have a board game with a boy named Angie anyhow. Not everybody in America lives in a town that's half Italian. They don't even know that boys can have names like Angelo. Like when I visited Miami, I met a boy named Jesus. He was cute too.

But you can't run around putting Jesus on your list of romantic boys."

I sighed. "Let's not worry about everybody in America. Let's make the game just for us."

"Think big," said Megan. "Market it nationally."

Market it?

"Let's not use names from the basketball team after all," said Faith. "Let's pick out romantic names." Faith smiled happily, remembering romance plots and heroes who swung their women up on horses and took them to exotic locales and rescued them from danger. "Dirk," said Faith. "Lance. Brandon. Nicholas." She batted her eyelashes. Faith has wonderful eyes. Very large, sunk so there's lots of room for various shades of eye shadow. Long naturally dark lashes that sweep her cheeks just like a romance book cover heroine's.

"Real people," said Megan scornfully, "are not named Dirk. Let's go all-American. Christopher. Michael. David."

I know a dozen Michaels, and I never tire of the name. I think it's beautiful. I added another square to the Monopoly board and called it Michael. I gave him 9. Might as well have high stakes.

"Stephen," continued Megan, making her own squares now. "Josh. Mark. Alexander. Stanley."

"Stanley?" Faith demanded.

"I used to have a cat named Stanley," explained Megan. "We got him from the shelter and that was the name he came with. They were named alphabetically, like hurricanes."

Faith tore Stanley off the board. "Stanley is not a romantic name. I refuse to have him. With my luck I'd win Stanley and you'd win Lance."

Megan threw her Scottie dog at Faith.

Faith flung her iron at Megan.

"What are you two doing?" I said. "Fighting over Stanley? Stanley doesn't exist."

"Sorry," said Megan, handing the pieces back to Faith to set back down on GO. "I was just excited. I react that way to boys." She started counting out money.

"We're not going to buy the boys," said Faith.

"No, but we'll need cash for our dates," said Megan. "My dates are going to be expensive. I'm expecting jet planes and five-star restaurants. And no bouquets of roses. I want diamonds."

I stared at my Monopoly board until my eyes went out of focus. The solid square of utilities and avenues shifted position and condensed, getting softer and rounder. My game board would not have right angles and sharp turns. It would be hearts. Perhaps a series of interlocking hearts.

GO TO JAIL turned to lace and love.

INCOME TAX became holding hands and candlelight.

PENNSYLVANIA RAILROAD was flowers and chocolates.

I saw lettering: curlicues of antique script with hearts and flowers intertwined. Initials carved on trees. Notes on handmade paper and sweet secret messages on tiny cell phone screens.

I saw romantic moments. Exchanges of the little prizes from the bottoms of cereal boxes and exchanges of gold bracelets engraved with names. Drives in the backseats of stretch limousines and drives in the front seats of fabulous sports cars. Balloon bouquets arriving at front doors and laughing couples airborne in hot-air balloon baskets. Sweet soft waltzes with one head on one shoulder, and hard, pounding crowds screaming at bands singing that one special song.

"I'll invent Romance: The Game of Love," I said. It would be pink. Several shades of pink, rosy like the dawn of love. Perhaps the board itself would be scented.

"I don't know," said Megan. "I think this is stupid. I'd rather play Monopoly, where at least you know what you're after. With boys, who knows? And we can't invent a board game of romance, because how would you win? How would you know when you ever got to the end of the game? What exactly is it that you'd win?"

My board was now a mishmash of computer paper, bad drawings and overlapping strips of tape. Only in my mind was it laced with romance.

"I'm going home," said Megan. "I may call Jimmy up and yell at him till I feel better."

Faith slid off the bed. "I'm tired myself. I'll see you tomorrow, Kelly." She stretched, yawned and stretched again. She started to put away the Monopoly pieces for me but I put my fingertips on the board and held it down against the denim spread. I was still thinking.

They had become bored as fast as they'd gotten interested, but that was because I didn't have a game yet, just an idea. They couldn't go far on ideas; they had to have the real thing. But maybe I could give it to them.

Romance: The Game of Love.

Megan had asked the right thing. What would you win?

What does anybody want to win?

Happily Ever After.

CHAPTER

Ms. Simms stood in front of her sociology students in her usual peculiar posture, left hand cupped beneath her right elbow, so her right arm was propped toward the ceiling. In this hand, she held her lecture notes, precisely angled to block her face from the class. She is the only teacher I have ever had who writes out what she plans to say.

"I just wish her notes could block out her voice as well," Angie muttered.

Poor Ms. Simms has a voice pitched too high. She sounds like a six-year-old, but she's about my parents' age, and hefty. Even after all these months of lectures—she has a great deal of information she is desperate to impart—I'm startled when that squeaking voice emerges from that massive chest.

"She's not so bad," whispered Faith.

Angie rolled his dark eyes. "She's too intense for me. I like laid-back people."

Our row, from door to windows, has Wendy, empty seat, me, Faith and Angie. Faith sat with her knees turned to the window so she could watch Angie all period long. She was pretty obvious about it. Angie had never noticed.

Ms. Simms lowered her cupped elbow fractionally and peered around the class. "Angelo?" she screeched. "Is that you talking?"

Angie is one of those people with the perfect name, like a policeman named Copp or a surgeon named Cutter. He is the angel of his first and last names. "I'm sorry, Ms. Simms." The smile had its usual effect. Ms. Simms raised her elbow and vanished again behind her notes. Faith sighed longingly over the smile not directed at her.

"I am opposed to people who call me Angelo," murmured Angie, more or less in Faith's direction. "I wish I had a real name."

Faith was close enough to touch his tight dark curls. I knew how much she wanted to. "How about Dirk?" she suggested. "Or Lance?"

Angie lit up. "Dirk," he breathed. "It's me. Can't you see me on my mission, screwing the silencer on my weapon as I prepare to vanquish the enemy?"

"Perfectly," said Faith. "Next to you is a beautiful blonde filled with adoration."

Angie put on a tough but carefree expression and began scanning a distant horizon for possible national enemies. Faith choked back a giggle. Angie continued performing for her. She had certainly overdosed on romance books if she was telling Angie to have a beautiful blonde next to him. Faith has dark hair.

I had dice in my purse. I hadn't told Faith, who had apparently forgotten about our original little romance game. But I had not forgotten. Sociology was the right setting. Sweet, oblivious Angie. Terrific Jeep. Conceited Will. Losers Chuckie, Kenny and Avery. Various ordinary types to fill the other squares.

The game would be my own indoor activity. Playable only during sociology.

A secret.

Unless, of course, I rolled Jeep and won the plays on the squares, and Jeep asked me out, and Wendy got jealous, and I was the Queen of Romance. Then I wouldn't keep it a secret. I would laugh and toss my gold-ribbon hair and know I had truly reached Happily Ever After.

Ms. Simms was talking about quizzes, but not the usual sort with a grade. It was just another of her weird weekend assignments. Each of us was to design a quiz for the rest of the class to take. "Statistically correct," she said. "Data to be interpreted in a reasonable fashion. Controls that can be measured."

Nobody was listening to her. That's what sociology is at Cummington High. A forty-five-minute stretch of not listening. That's why it was a perfect place for my romance game.

"I like this, Faith," said Angie. "I'll even let you sit with me at lunch if you'll tell me more about Dirk and his beautiful blonde."

Across the empty desk next to me, Wendy was perking up. Wendy rarely participates in sociology because she despises Ms. Simms. But she's always on the lookout for material for her soap opera. That is what she always told Parker. "Material," she'd say intensely. "Let's go find material." Then they would vanish for three hours in Mother's car. At night. My father muttered, "I bet I know what kind of material they're finding, all right." "Don't tell me about it," said my mother, who is of the old school of parenting: What you don't know cannot hurt you. My mother is a great believer in wrapping yourself in cotton wool. Not that she ever has to wrap herself. My father is a great believer in protecting her. He provides the cotton wool, she shrinks inside it and they're both happy.

I felt around in my purse for the dice.

"And the quiz you devise may be on any subject whatsoever," said Ms. Simms, "but it must have questions each of us in this classroom can answer. We will then compile responses and get a clear profile of our own class."

"Anything whatsoever?" repeated Will. "Like . . . how many of us prefer imported to domestic chocolate? Which of us are abused by our parents?"

Everybody but Faith laughed. She was too busy being

thrilled about sitting with Angie at lunch. I was pretty thrilled for her. It was truly romantic: naming a romance name and winning the best boy, the one you've always yearned for. I couldn't quite believe it. Neither could Wendy, who was leaning forward to catch whatever Angie was saying next to Faith.

"Excellent suggestions, Will!" cried Ms. Simms. She was so excited, she lowered her elbow. "A series of questions designed to glean statistics on child abuse right in our room. Now, that will be meaningful."

"Some of us might decline to answer," Jeep pointed out.

Will laughed. "Then the rest of us will know that under your sweatshirt, you're covered with bruises."

Jeep grinned at Will, and Will grinned at Jeep. Probably the only time all week Will would do that. Normal emotions came second to conceit in Will. "I am covered with bruises," said Jeep. "It's my fellow basketball players. They beat up on me. I've been meaning to report it to the proper authorities but Will pays them off."

Will finished grinning, which for him was a short-term exercise. Now he was just bony and snobbish. If he ever grinned at me the way he had at Jeep, I'd know that I possessed a million dollars Will needed in five minutes.

I rolled one of the dice gently across the surface of my desk.

It rolled off onto the floor, making a tiny clatter, and kept on rolling away from me. I couldn't believe it. One limp toss and the dumb thing was gone forever under Will's desk.

Will heard the faint rattle, frowned slightly and bent over to retrieve the die.

He looked around to see where it had come from. When Ms. Simms wasn't looking, I signaled him. Will narrowed his eyes at me. I nodded, *Yes, that's really mine; yes, I want it back.*

Will got up, strolled back to me and handed it over.

"Will?" said Ms. Simms.

"Just giving Kelly back her die," said Will.

"Oh," said Ms. Simms.

"I want to do chocolate," said Faith quickly. "My quiz will establish how many of us cannot get through a day without chocolate. My theory is that it will be ninety-five percent of us."

"I want every quiz to have twenty questions," said Ms. Simms. "Faith, limiting yourself to chocolate could pose problems. Perhaps you could expand your questionnaire to include, say, food allergies."

Angie clutched his chest and patted his heart with excitement. "That does sound intriguing, Ms. Simms. I can hardly wait to find out who gets hives."

Faith lowered her lashes at him. "I do. Every time I think about you, Angie, I get a rash."

The class howled with laughter.

Wendy was writing it all down. Before long, we would hear this dialogue over the public-address system. Not everybody in class would recognize themselves, because Wendy is pretty clever at disguising lines. But her soap opera would not really be original. That's the sort of thing I comfort myself with when I think that Wendy is about four hundred times more creative than I am, and probably I should give up right now.

This time I rolled my die very very very gently, and I quickly lowered my arms to make little walls to catch the die if it tried anything sneaky.

It was a five.

I glanced at vertical row five.

Kenny, Will, Angie, Margaret and Susan.

If I rolled a six next, I'd have to start over. There was no sixth seat.

If I rolled a four or five, I'd have to start over. I was not going to play my indoor game of romance with a girl. Even though I quite like Margaret, and Susan has a nice car.

The other three were a good representation of the class. Kenny: totally disgusting. Will: totally conceited. Angie: a perfect person with whom my best friend was going to have lunch. Just like life.

I rolled again.

For a moment, I didn't want to look at the dots that were showing. I giggled softly to myself instead. It's a habit I'm aware of, and I try to stop myself because I know how odd I must look: Kelly, entertained by nothing at all. Laughing into thin air like somebody due for a long stay on a psych ward.

I looked around to see if anybody had spotted me laughing. Everybody but Will was still laughing over Angie and Faith and the rash.

Will, however, was staring at me as if he rarely came across a human being so peculiar. I smiled. He looked away.

Now I lowered my eyes and saw the die, and there staring back at me were two little black dots.

Two.

Will was two.

Impossible not to laugh again. Impossible not to look at Will, who was so unlikely ever to have a romance with me. So I smiled once more, realizing even as the smile touched my lips that that was square one of my own game design. Smile at him.

Will smiled back. A real smile. As if he was a real person and not just a tall thin piece of cardboard labeled CONCEIT.

I ducked my head. My hair fell forward, slippery and straight, hiding me from everyone including Will.

You're turning chicken, I told myself. Hiding is not one of the squares. The rules are notice him, talk to him, sit next to him.

But in the grand old tradition of school, I was saved by the bell. Basketball players charged out as if they were on the court.

Wendy said, in a high, attention-getting voice, "I think that's at least two episodes, don't you?"

In study hall, I thought about Ms. Simms's assignment. Food allergy quizzes. Child abuse quizzes. Boring.

Let them have their rashes and bruises. I would undertake love. I would do a romance quiz. After all, I hadn't thought of anything except romance since I folded up my Monopoly game and began drawing interlocking hearts on the poster board I had finally located behind my computer desk.

So far, I had a Start Heart, three Dating Hearts and a Happily Ever After Heart.

At first I tried to define Happily Ever After, but I gave up. Who knows what Happily Ever After means to somebody else? A father for your children? A cocaptain for your yacht? A partner for earning your first million? A companion with whom to wander in flowery meadows?

I would have to leave Happily Ever After blank.

Okay. A romance quiz. Get on it, Kelly, I ordered myself. How about pairs? Circle which is more romantic: roses or dandelions. Satin or denim. Horse-drawn carriages or escalators.

But that was as dull as food allergies. Anybody would check off *satin* before *denim*. I needed a quiz that would force people to think. I began listing words and phrases.

Stars. Snuggling. Earrings. Perfume. Midnight blue. City skyline. Dark eyes.

Those seemed fairly romantic. Words for the cover of a thick historical novel or the backdrop of a slick magazine advertisement.

Now some words that were not romantic.

Smoking. Tacos. Compost.

And words that weren't much of anything.

Clock. Envelope. Kneecap.

Maybe the quiz taker would give each word a numerical rating, one to ten. Which words were most likely to make a person think of romance? And the person taking the quiz would have to check off boy or girl because maybe some words meant more to boys than to girls, although personally I had seen little sign that boys had any words on their romance list.

My last class of the day is American history. It was January, so we had passed the Civil War and were steaming on toward the Last Frontier. I had not read the chapter. Once my mother told me that if I put one-tenth the effort into school that I put into complaining about not knowing any boys, I'd at least be able to go to a good college where there are lots of good boys to put an effort into. She's right, of course. The thing is, I can't seem to get into studying. It lacks a certain something.

Boys, I guess.

I know I could study with some terrific boy sharing the desk.

Oh well.

Faith sat down next to me. She was so deep in her crush on Angie, she could hardly focus. Toothpaste was never marketed by a wider, whiter smile than Faith gave me as she dropped her history text onto the desk. "Kelly," she whispered.

“Yes, Faith.” I have sat with her through many an agonizing crush. I estimate that Faith runs about four serious crushes a year. Each one hurts her. It’s so unfair that love, of all things, can be so painful.

“Do you think he’ll ask me out, Kelly? Lunch was just great. We laughed steadily. I mean, he’d have to want to do that again, wouldn’t he?”

Fluffy brown hair circled her eager face. She has a face that makes the rest of us happy. A smile you have to reflect with one of your own. A sweet person, a good person. Had Angie seen this?

Faith shook her head twice, denying the possibility, and then nodded twice, believing that it might really happen.

“Got a twitch, Faith?” said Will, striding to his seat without waiting for an answer. We didn’t answer him either. From experience we knew he wouldn’t be looking our way again, because he didn’t intend to talk to us anyhow. He just meant to demonstrate his superiority with a wisecrack and then ignore us.

What if Angie does ask Faith out? I thought. I will be the very last girl without a boyfriend. Like gym when they’re picking teams. I’ll be the one still sitting on the floor while everybody pities me and nobody wants me.

“The sun is in my eyes,” I croaked. “I’m changing seats.”

There was in fact a faint glint over by the windows. But I was moving to get control of myself before jealousy lodged in my heart. I refuse to feel jealousy toward my best friend. I slid into an empty seat.

Will looked up, startled.

Without planning, I had arrived at square four. Sit next to him.

I looked quickly away. Mrs. Weston wasn't saying anything interesting, so I opened my latest magazine underneath my textbook and flipped it open to the quiz. (I don't bother with a magazine unless it has quizzes. I love to fill things out.)

Test your intimacy quotient, it said.

Oh good. I always wondered what my intimacy quotient was.

1. You want to spend an afternoon with Geoff. Will you suggest

a. Frisbee tossing?

b. Looking at his baby pictures?

c. Making fudge?

d. Shopping at the mall?

2. He isn't paying enough attention to you. Do you decide

a. He's too worried about his SATs?

b. He likes another girl more?

c. He's gay?

d. He's getting the flu?

3. You just aren't close enough to the boy you love. Is it because

a. He isn't your ideal?

b. You're afraid of intimacy?

c. You can't relax with boys?

d. He doesn't like you enough to bother?

♥

I'd never give any answer suggested for question number one. But every answer for question number two and question number three was possible.

I concentrated. I decided Geoff and I would make fudge.

Mrs. Weston continued talking. I calculated my intimacy quotient when I had struggled through all twenty questions. My score was forty-seven. I flipped to the back of the magazine and looked up the meaning of the result.

Under 50, it said. *You have real problems relating to boys. Perhaps you should consider counseling.*

Counseling! I didn't need a mental health expert. I needed a boy to love me.

But even though I knew the quiz was stupid and the questions were stupid and the score was stupid and even though I was in public, I started crying.

Inside myself I froze, turning the tears solid, getting very still. I won't cry, I won't cry, I won't cry. I stopped, but not before a few tears trickled down my cheeks.

A large hand with freakishly long fingers landed on my magazine. Surely Mrs. Weston didn't have hands that big. Surely—

But it was Will, curling the magazine into a cylinder and removing it to his desk. Without unwrapping the magazine, he read the quiz, turning the roll like an axle to read the columns.

"What's your score?" he breathed.

I considered lying. I considered not answering. But Will was not worth it. "Forty-seven," I admitted.

Will grinned ear to ear. He didn't bother to face me. I only saw the grin in profile.

That's right, you bum, I thought. Laugh at me. I bet you got a thirty-three. The only thing you've ever been intimate with is a basketball.

A low intimacy quotient. What a thing to have in common.

The need to cry vanished. I felt thick and dull. The smile faded from Will's face. He returned the magazine. He didn't tell me his score and I didn't ask. I swiveled in my chair to see what Faith was making of my exchanges with Will.

Faith had not noticed. She had written *Faith Bennett Angelotti* six times in different scripts.

Feminist commentators may think that we girls are beyond this kind of thing, but they're wrong. We're still here shading our writing with our hands so nobody can see that we're trying out a boy's last name in case we get married.

Bells rang. Our final announcements come complete with

chords. Mrs. Weston finished her history lecture while the principal cleared his throat and school came to an end.

Our principal reads off a paper his secretary has printed out for him. Unfortunately his voice stops at the end of each line whether the sentence stops there or not. Drives me crazy.

"Drives me crazy," said Will.

Probably the highest intimacy quotient I'll have all week, I thought.

"Someday I'm going to put my fist through the sound system," said Will. But he wasn't talking to me or really to anybody. He was just thinking out loud. You didn't get a thirty-three, I thought. You got a zero.

"Put your fist through Dr. Scheider instead," advised somebody. "He deserves it more."

"Key Club will meet after school in order to discuss," said Dr. Scheider. He cleared his throat. An entire school twitched. "The fund-raiser for next year the Ecology Club has a field."

Pause, filled by Will breaking a pencil in half.

"Trip to the state capitol to meet our. Representative and the cost is twenty-seven dollars. Fifty cents the following students report to guidance office immediately after the final."

Several people were sticking four fingers at their mouths to indicate that on the gag scale, this was worse than usual. A four-finger gag is pretty serious.

"Bell the school sweatshirts in the new designs are in the school store."

Everybody shuddered but not even Will breathed a syllable of correction. We were all awaiting Wendy's broadcast. We are addicted to Wendy's soap. It usually runs two minutes. This week we were worrying about whether Greg would change his socks and whether Allegra was going to shave the right hemisphere of her skull and put safety pins through her eyebrows and quit school for the British rock star she was seeing. There was also the problem Brandon and Octavia were having. Brandon seemed to be falling in love with Lulu. Would Octavia kill Lulu or Brandon?

Wendy has a very intense voice, as if somebody is holding a gun to her head while she reads.

"Brandon slouches against the tall brick column in the library. His eyes drift past Allegra, for whom he has nothing but scorn, and land longingly on Octavia. No matter how drawn Brandon is to Lulu, Octavia has his heart. But Octavia is being cruel to him. 'Brandon,' says Octavia, lips curled, 'I want a real man with a real name. Dirk, perhaps. Or Lance. Someone on a mission, saving those he loves from certain doom. And you, Brandon, worry only about whether to have a cappuccino or a latte. Do I care about you? Do I care whether you have a Gucci jockstrap? No. Does your body or your mind—' "

And Wendy was off the air.

It had happened once before when Brandon and Octavia shacked up together. Dr. Scheider got rather fierce about that. I guess Dr. Scheider did not care to have Wendy mention jockstraps, even designer models, over the school sound system. Perhaps there were school board members in the building, something that did happen once or twice a year.

Everybody in my history class got a kick out of the silence, waiting to see if Wendy would come back on with a revised underwear statement. But she didn't. The next announcement was from a guidance counselor about a deadline for applying to something or other. It is a rule of mine never to listen to guidance counselors.

School was over.

Everyone raced out of class but I was fastest. Parker is allowed to drive Mom's car one day a week and this was the day. Parker tried hard to leave without me so he could be alone with Wendy. I sympathized with them but I'd rather be a pain than take the school bus. My romantic ideals apply more to me than to others.

The crosswalks were jammed with parents in cars coming for their kids. As I stood in the crowd waiting for a chance to rush to the parking lot, Wendy and my brother emerged hand in hand from the office complex, laughing. Whatever objection Dr. Scheider had to that episode, Wendy had won. Parker leaned down a little toward Wendy and she stretched up, and their heads rested against each other.

The person standing next to me sighed. It was Jeep, his eyes fastened on my brother and Wendy. His handsome mouth turned down sadly and his head tilted wearily. He still wanted to supply the shoulder on which Wendy rested.

Wendy never glanced our way. She was completely absorbed in Parker, and when they kissed, their intimacy quotient was as high as it gets. Jeep sighed again. He didn't glance my way either. Whatever Wendy had, I did not.

But what did I expect? Me with my intimacy quotient of forty-seven? Me in need of professional help because I couldn't relate to boys? Did I really think Jeep would spot me and suddenly forget all about Wendy and want only me?

I reached our car just as Park and Wendy did.

Wendy glared at me. Did the little sister have to show up right now? Couldn't she just drop dead somewhere?

"I could drive," I offered brightly. "Then you could have the backseat."

"No," said Parker firmly. "The backseat is your territory, kid. Always has been, always will be."

Kid? He was ten months older.

He opened the front door for Wendy. I got in back by myself.

This is my life, I thought. Alone in the backseat. When I sighed heavily, nobody heard. Parker and Wendy were having their pre-driving-out-of-the-parking-lot kiss.

On the great board game of Romance, I was still on square one.

CHAPTER

Interlocked hearts are hard.

They have dead ends. You can't get your players from one heart to the next. If you add connector strips, you get this jumble of left and right turns and you can't tell where to go next, and now they don't even look like hearts, but really bad interstate systems.

My original attempt of six interlocked hearts turned into gridlock. It was a traffic jam instead of a game.

My second design had six hearts facing in a circle, points to the center, attached by slender ribbons. You swung around each heart and over the ribbon to the next heart. My hearts looked like apples drawn by a kindergartner with visual problems.

My third design was one enormous heart with four

layers. You circled the heart first on the red path, then the rose path, then the pink and finally bridal white. It was fun to color. I divided each path into one-inch squares, which I would label for action or dates or something.

I counted up the squares. Sixty per path for a total of two hundred forty squares. I had to think up two hundred forty romantic events?

Even my mother and father, with all those years of romance behind them, hadn't managed that. Most of their romance was repeat anyway—the usual flowers, dinner out and Hallmark cards. But that was three. Only two hundred thirty-seven to go.

I did my sketching in the back of my history notebook.

Faith had to watch basketball practice because now that Angie had had lunch with her, she figured she was a member of the team. The coach is pretty loose about kids sitting on the bleachers. You just have to stay quiet. There are usually at least a dozen kids lounging around, half watching and half in a stupor from school.

We sat on the top bleacher so we could rest our backs against the wall. The poor boys, fourteen of them, were being subjected to various forms of torture. Right now they were running like madmen toward the opposite gym wall, hurling themselves feetfirst against it and using the leap to turn around and race back.

It's one thing to do that in a swimming pool. The water will catch you if you fall. You're not going to break your neck, twist your ankle or crack your ribs. It was good I had my Romance game to design. I could stop watching the boys playing suicide with their bones and concentrate on hearts.

Kenny—he of mega-loser fame—is a scorekeeper. He wanders in and out of all athletic activities, on the fringes of these as of everything else, and today after wandering over to the coaches, he wandered up to us. "Hello, Kenny," said Faith in an unwelcoming voice.

Kenny, who perhaps brushes his teeth on a monthly basis and last replaced his shirt in seventh grade, smiled and said, "Hi, Faith. Hi, Kell. What's new?"

I detest this question. You immediately start to wonder what *is* new in your life and of course *nothing* is new in your life; it's the same old routine. Or if there is something new, you don't want to tell Kenny about it. Why couldn't he just say "How ya doin'?" like a normal person, so you could say "Fine" and be done with it?

Of course, Faith did have something new and wonderful in her life. Angie. She took a deep happy breath because she was dying to talk all about it. But once her lungs were full, she remembered that nothing had happened yet and something might go wrong and did she really want to boast about it before the event? Then she looked hard at Kenny and realized she had been about to discuss an actual personal emotion with him, so she let the air out of her lungs again and pretended to be excited about the team exercises.

Kenny is used to being left out and he knew he was being left out of whatever Faith had meant to say, so he looked my way for a response. I was flipping pages in my spiral notebook to hide my heart sketches. Kenny's hand flew out and slid between the pages to flip back to whatever I'd been hiding.

"Hearts," said Kenny slowly.

I would have ripped my notebook away but the pages would have been torn.

"Hearts," he repeated thoughtfully. "You've never come to basketball practice, Kelly. Today you come. Today you sit drawing little hearts and trying to hide them. Today you changed seats to be next to Will. Then you and Will talked." Kenny smiled. "So that's it, huh? You're crazy in love with Will, aren't you?"

"I am not. I am just drawing shapes. I happen to like hearts."

"'Cause you're in love," agreed Kenny.

"I am not in love. These hearts have nothing to do with Will. I'm just—I'm—well—playing a game."

Kenny laughed. "That's what love is, they say. A game. But more fun with two players. Hey, does Will know?"

"No!" I screamed. "You're wrong!"

The coach looked up at me and glared.

The entire basketball team looked up at me and glared.

I shrank down into my seat, making little apology faces, and Kenny stood below me laughing. "Guess I'll tell Will, then." He bounded down the bleachers, trotted across the gym floor, narrowly missing death by trampling, and sat on the bench next to the water bottles. Sooner or later, Will would go get a squirt of water.

"I'm going to die," I informed Faith.

Faith flipped my spiral notebook open herself and frowned at my hearts. "Is Kenny right? Are you in love with Will?"

"No!"

I wonder why we always deny love. I remember in middle school, if you were accused of the crime of loving, you screamed denials constantly and stopped ever even looking at the boy you were accused of liking. The boys could destroy each other by yodeling, "An-drew lo-oves Jen-nie," and both Andrew and Jennie would flinch and blush.

Love is this great thing that most songs and books and poems and lives are all about. So the minute we actually think there might be love around, we start laughing and pretending and hiding from it.

I was hiding my hearts under the cover of my notebook.

If I really do fall in love one day, I thought, will I hide it? What happens if you hide love so well, the person you love thinks you don't care? How come you can't just walk up to somebody and say, You know what? I love you.

Faith said, "Kenny just told Will. Look over there."

I made the mistake of looking over there. Will had a large bottle of water and had been squirting it into his mouth from a distance. Startled by Kenny's message, Will squirted without swallowing. Water spewed over his face, ran down onto his chest and spilled on the floor.

Kenny tossed a towel over the spill.

Will, staring at us, wiped his face with his arm.

Actually, he must have been staring at me, but we were too far away to see his eyes and I felt safer thinking it was both of us drawing Will's attention.

Will waved.

"Wave back," whispered Faith. "Don't be such a lump, Kelly. Take action!"

I waved back.

Will jogged onto the court to rejoin the action.

"I have to get out of here," I said.

"Why? He waved at you!"

"Faith, I don't even like Will."

"Then why are you drawing the hearts?"

"Faith!"

"Just testing," she said, leaning all over me like a cat wanting its chin scratched. "I think waving back is a good sign. There are possibilities here. It would be fun to have me date Angie while you date Will. We'd have two-fifths of the starting basketball team sewn up."

I moaned and took the late bus home before practice ended. Before I had to think about dealing with Will.

"Oh, George, you shouldn't have!" cried my mother, taking her tiny wrapped gift with delight. This time my father had brought a white lace bookmark, six inches long, an inch wide: thread spun into a row of hearts.

Nobody ever spun a row of hearts for me.

Members of the opposite sex! I thought. Report to my house. Gift in hand. Kiss on lips.

"That's lovely, Mother," I said enthusiastically. I gave Daddy a hug. "You're such a sweetie," I told him. "I should be so lucky."

He shared hugs with Mother and me. "Your time will come, Kelly. I don't mind if it's slow arriving. I kind of like my baby girl."

I minded.

"Let's go out for dinner," said Daddy, exclusively to Mom.

"Oh, George. I've already started dinner. I've been marinating the chicken since this morning and the rice is a special—"

"It'll be good tomorrow. Come on. Where shall we go? The Japanese restaurant on Fifth? The Sicilian place over by the campus? What are you in the mood for?" This triggered Daddy's musical memory and he began loudly singing "I'm in the Mood for Love." My father has a terrible voice and worse rhythm.

I was glad Parker wasn't home yet. He always ruins it by telling Dad, "If you can't reach the notes, don't sing the song."

Details, details.

Sometimes we go out as a family but more often my parents go out alone. Megan says this is abnormal, because once you have children, you are obligated to take them with you wherever you go. Especially if you're going to a nice restaurant. Megan says my parents are selfish. I say they're romantic and Megan is jealous.

Parker came bounding in, saw Mom looking for her heavy coat and said, "You're going out? In Dad's car? Then I can keep Mom's car and drive Wendy?"

"May I," corrected Mom.

"Where with Wendy?" said Dad.

"May I," said Parker to Mom. "Don't know," he said to Dad.

My father looked steadily at my brother. Parker looked steadily back. They didn't take their eyes off each other, a contest I didn't understand and Mom didn't see because she was humming around getting ready for her date. Whatever the contest was, Parker won. My father dropped his eyes, grinned at nothing and said, "You have enough money, son?"

"Could use more."

Dad gave him some bills, folded over so I couldn't tell how much, and Park was gone. Dad held Mom's coat for her. "You going to be all right alone, Kelly?"

They hated worrying about me when they were out, so I said, as I always did, "Sure."

Daddy touched the earrings he'd given my mother at some anniversary, tiny silver violets, and the silver necklace that was last year's Christmas gift. "You're beautiful, Vi," he said softly.

My mother lit up, the way she does for compliments, and for one moment she really was beautiful.

They left hand in hand.

In the TV room I slid a rented movie into the VCR and went back to the kitchen to pop popcorn. Then I settled in front of the computer screen to compose my sociology quizzes. I can't actually do more than one thing at a time, but I do love to think of myself as a multitasker.

My current plan was to have a hundred words everybody would check off for romantic value. But when I finished (lace, calorie counting, candlelight, wallpaper), it was obvious that everybody would check off the same words I did and nobody would learn a thing, which didn't meet the requirements of Ms. Simms.

Next I tried categories.

♥

FOODS	COLORS	CARS	HOBBIES	PLACES
chocolate	scarlet	SUV	holding hands	McDonald's
cough drops	royal blue	Porsche	tennis	ski resort
carrot sticks	black	Harley	bowling	campgrounds
wedding cake	avocado	limousine	hitchhiking	Disney World

Colors might be interesting. Maybe there was a person who would think avocado was a romantic hue. But who would check off cough drops under FOODS? And who would put hitchhiking ahead of holding hands under HOBBIES?

I munched popcorn. I got butter on my paper.

Was Faith on the phone with Angie?

Were they arranging their first real date?

Would everything work out for them?

Or would Faith report back that she was right about F names and that people who wore them were doomed to a fat, frumpy, failed life?

"That's it!" I cried. "A name game!"

I'd list names. Which is more romantic? Ethel or Rosemary? Laura or LuEllen? Starr or Stephanie?

By the time the movie was over, I had written two tests.

♥

Kelly Williams~Sociology w/ Ms. Simms

ASSIGNMENT: quiz **TOPIC:** romance

In this quiz, we will find out what words or phrases make boys think of romance and what words or phrases make girls think of romance. You may check no more than ten words on this list.

WORD	BOY	GIRL
chocolate		
kitten		
dancing		
violin		
smoking		
flowers		
whipped cream		
tennis		
city skyline		
fame		
midnight blue		
sunset		
snuggling		
novels		
high heels		
sweatpants		
rings		
stockings		
sparkles		
fragrance		
ruffles		
sneaker laces		

WORD	BOY	GIRL
strapless		
boots		
drumbeats		
candlelight		
plaid		
eye shadow		
laughter		
stars		
patchwork quilt		
Fourth of July		
lavender		
dark eyes		
diamonds		
velvet		
lilac		
tennis		
beaches		
silver		
snow		

♥

Kelly Williams~Sociology w/ Ms. Simms
QUIZ ASSIGNMENT №2

In this quiz, we'll find out if certain names automatically make a person feel romantically disposed or turn a person off. Give each name a romantic rating by checking a column to the right.

NAME	VERY ROMANTIC	RATHER ROMANTIC	NOT VERY ROMANTIC	TOTALLY UNROMANTIC
Amanda				
Adam				
Barbara				
Nigel				
Emily				
Michael				
Jasmine				
Aiden				
Gwendolyn				
Scott				
Heather				
Kelsey				
Joshua				
Glenn				
Alexis				
Tatiana				
Patrick				

Christina

Rudy

Nellie

Cameron

Wanda

Henry

Paulette

Dominic

Ashley

Brayden

Anthony

Holly

Annabelle

Jessica

Max

Sean

Brianna

Ethan

Madison

I went to bed laughing. For once I had had a day packed with romance. Of course, it wasn't real. Other people were doing it while I was writing it, but it turned out that romance is fun even on paper.

Good night, world, I thought. I hope you're ready for me. Because I'm about to leave square one.

CHAPTER

I cannot now believe that I turned in those quizzes.

You would think sixteen years of life would have taught me to avoid public humiliation.

But no.

I ran toward humiliation as if it were male and in love with me.

In sociology, Faith's eyes were fastened on Angie.

Angie's eyes were fastened on his desk, where he kept putting things he could stare at. First his pen, then his book, then a paper clip, then four quarters he stacked and

restacked, as if playing a single person's shell game. His cheeks were flushed, and against his olive skin, the ruddy color was unexpected and beautiful.

I convinced myself, against a lot of previous evidence, that Angie was in love and, furthermore, in love with Faith, but too shy to glance at her under the stress of powerful emotion.

"All right, class," piped Ms. Simms. "Pass in your quizzes."

Each of us handed the homework down the row to the person in front, who would stack the papers and hand them to the left, until the front left desk had acquired all the papers and handed them neatly to Ms. Simms.

Fatal.

Honey sits two seats in front of me. When she covered her quiz with mine, she glanced down at what I had written. Staring into my pages, she yelled, "Listen! Listen, you guys!" She was laughing so hard, she had to whack the top of her desk with her palm. "You will never in a million years guess what Kelly did her quiz on!" She turned in her seat to laugh at me, taking the opportunity to cast her emerald green eyes over Jeep and Will and Angie. Last year her eyes were plain old hazel but she got tinted contacts and now her eyes are truly remarkable. To look at Honey is to be dazzled.

"What?" said Jeep, leaning way over his desk to catch a glimpse of my topic.

The entire rest of the class imitated him, leaning way over their desks too. Faith frowned at me, with no idea what was coming. We'd talked so much about Angie that I had forgotten to share my quizzes with her.

Naturally Honey adored having so many fine people lean her way. "Romance," she said in a low sexy voice. "Kelly wrote not one but two tests for us to take to see if we're romantic." She pointed a long thin mocking finger at me. Every eye in class followed the tip of her finger and focused on me.

"I don't think you took this assignment seriously, Kelly," said Ms. Simms. "I will be distressed if you simply imitated some foolish nonsense out of *Cosmopolitan*."

"Kelly is serious," said Honey. "She takes romance very seriously." Honey paused for drama. She's as good as Wendy. "Kelly is always studying those of us who possess romance."

I could not even duck my head and let my hair waterfall over my face. I had to sit there laughing and pretending to join in the fun. I would be lucky if I kept from crying.

"That's cool," said Jeep. "Let's take the romance quizzes first."

There was nowhere safe to look. Ahead of me was Honey's pointing finger. To my left was Will. To my right, Wendy. I picked out a space and fixed my eyes on the blankness as if behind the thin air stood God or my guardian angel. *Rescue me*, I said. *Don't let this be happening*.

"Actually this will be rather interesting," said Ms. Simms, glancing through my quizzes. "We'll find out whether boys and girls agree that certain words signal romance."

"We have most of the period left, Ms. Simms," said Jeep in a pleasant cooperative voice. "Why don't I just run down to the office, run off twenty copies of each, and we'll take the quizzes right now?"

"Good idea," said another boy. "I'm in a real rush to know if I'm romantic or not."

"You're not," the boys assured him. "You're a loser."

"You could take lessons from me if you want," Angie offered generously.

"You? Angie, the girls never go out with you twice. It'd have to be a quick lesson."

"You mean I never go out with a girl twice," Angie corrected. "I've got high standards."

I risked a glance at Faith. But she was not upset. She was wreathed in smiles. She knew she met those high standards.

Jeep stood up and took the quizzes from an unprotesting Ms. Simms. He was back in no time to pass the papers out. He was already laughing. "Wait till you read this, guys," he warned everybody.

"Take this seriously," cautioned Ms. Simms.

Everybody laughed raucously.

I wondered if a person could blush to death. Perhaps my death certificate would read, *Overheating from blushing caused her central nervous system to—*

"Because," said Ms. Simms, and her squeaky voice suddenly dropped an octave into normalcy, "to love and to be loved are the greatest joys on earth."

There was complete silence.

It was a truth. More than we'd ever learn in science or math or history.

But who can tolerate the truth? Especially in front of her friends?

People wrote their names obediently at the top of their quiz sheets. They began reading the directions. Laughter began to riffle over the room, little brooks of giggles becoming torrents.

"Whipped cream?" said Angie. "*Whipped cream*, Kelly?"

I'll go live with Grandma, I thought. I'll never set foot in Cummington again.

"Chocolate, kitten, dancing, violin," read Honey. "Does anybody think that Kelly is just a little bit deprived?"

"Boots," read Kenny. "I don't see my other romantic favorites here, Kelly. Where is my leather? My whips?"

"Class!" cried Ms. Simms in her tiny pitiful scream. Brief silence settled. But the laughter had not vanished, just been muffled. "You're all envious of Kelly," said Ms. Simms. "She has sufficient character to attack the important parts of life. What you care about and dream about and struggle toward. Match her bravery with your honesty."

For a minute I thought she had saved me. I was able to breathe in without that jagged edge that is the start of tears. I let go of my pencil a little and released the cramps forming in my hand.

And Will said, "Crap." The single syllable was fierce and angry. "Flowers? Sparkles? Velvet? None of that has anything to do with love. This is stupid, Kelly. Love is promises. Generosity. Sharing. Forgiveness. Listening. Kindness. Love is important." Will looked at me with contempt. "Every single thing you've listed is shallow and stupid."

Of all people to say this—Will. He was right. The quiz was shallow and I was shallow. After all, I was the one with the intimacy quotient of forty-seven.

Of all people, it was Wendy who stepped up to the plate to save me. "Will," she said, "Kelly did not write a quiz on love. She wrote a quiz on romance. What's so bad about romance? Romance is the backdrop to love. Don't be so high and mighty. If you'd relax a little, you might have romance in your life too, instead of sweatpants and sneaker laces."

Will looked uncomfortable. "I guess I see what you mean," he said finally.

"Of course you do," said Wendy. "Romance is soft music and sleek cars. Holding hands and pretty dresses. Love is none of those. Love is profound and vast, not mere objects and textures. But romance is half the fun, Will."

For a moment, the entire class was caught up in Wendy's voice. We shared faraway looks and the dream was almost visible. *Let me have love*.

"That's interesting from you, Wendy," said Honey. "So let's see, Parker's car—the one he has to borrow one day a week—isn't sleek. And Jeep's car—the one he owns—is sleek. I guess you and Jeep were all romance and no love, huh, Wendy?"

Jeep didn't blush and fade like me. He simply ceased to breathe or be there.

Half the class attacked Honey for Jeep's sake. Ms. Simms had to yell for quiet but quiet never came. Even when the final bell rang, we were still saying ugly things and taking sides and stabbing each other.

What is this thing called love, I wondered, that turned this dull group into an emotional mob?

I got up last, wanting to see nobody, talk to nobody, be reminded of nobody. Wanting to be dead, actually, but there was an important test next class that I couldn't skip.

Will held the door for me.

"Thank you," I mumbled, stumbling through it, hating him for being there.

"Romantic of me, wasn't it?" he said sarcastically. As if doing romantic things were bad. He faked a smile and I had to tell him what his smile was like. "You've got a smile like an attack dog," I said.

We stood a moment staring at each other. I was so drained, I could hardly raise my chin, and looking up at the basketball player who was a star because of his inches required considerable raising of the chin.

"But you," he said softly, "have the smile of a pixie."

CHAPTER 5

A pixie?

Now, what, exactly, is a pixie?

I think of a feathery elf with button features who is fluttering on gauze wings among magic toadstools.

At home I stared at myself in the hall mirror. The day's blush had finally faded and I could see my features again. I do have a perky nose and a small chin. Is a pixie smile a good thing? Was Will being sarcastic when he held the door for me or did I read that into his voice because I was so upset?

"I don't want to wonder!" I cried aloud. "I want something to happen!"

I sagged into a chair. In the next room, my parents were

making supper, Mom chopping onions for spaghetti sauce while Dad minced garlic. He was teasing her.

There is romance, I reminded myself. I'm a witness.

I flung myself onto the sofa and began to cry and Parker came in.

That's the way it is with families and classrooms. No privacy. Always somebody watching.

"What's the matter?" said Park. He didn't come sit next to me or hug me. We aren't physically close, Parker and I. He did stand in the door, though, and wait patiently for an answer.

I shrugged.

"Has to be something," he said. "Maybe I can help."

The last thing I would ever do was admit what had happened in sociology. Or describe my romance game or Will or my feelings about life in general. Especially to Park, who didn't know any more than the rest of us did why Wendy liked him. "I was thinking of Mother and Daddy," I lied. "How romantic they are. Did you see the little heart bookmark?"

"Romantic?" said Park irritably. "Garbage. There's nothing romantic about that or about them either."

"Nothing romantic?" I repeated.

"He doesn't bring those presents because it's romantic. Don't you know anything, Kelly? He's just spreading oil on the waters."

"What waters?"

"Of their marriage. It's such a dumb marriage. I'm never going to have a fake marriage like theirs."

I was outraged. "A fake?" I sputtered. "Mother and Daddy?"

"They've been married eighteen years and any fool can tell Dad adores Mom, but she's so insecure, he has to go through this endless charade of proving himself week after week, year after year, gift after gift, bookmark after bookmark, flower after flower."

I could not think of my own mother as insecure. Insecure is a word for kids. Mothers are solid.

"And all because of Ellen, who could be dead now for all we know."

"*Ellen?*" I said. "Dad's high school girlfriend?"

We'd heard all about Ellen. She shared eight years of Daddy's life. His first car. His first trip to Europe. His first plane ride. His first weekend in New York. His first time on the West Coast. All with Ellen. Right after college, Ellen jilted Dad. Just up and said good-bye. Have you met somebody else? my father said. No, replied Ellen, I just don't want to spend my life with you.

Dad was shattered for about a month but then he met Mother and the romance of the century began between them.

"What could Ellen have to do with anything?" I said crossly. If Parker was going to make up some cheap story about how Daddy was really having an affair with Ellen on the side, I would kill him.

"Dad and Mom got married when they'd known each other six weeks. Talk about falling in love on the rebound.

Dad had been seeing Ellen for years. She was the first and only girl Dad ever dated. Dad worshiped Ellen. And less than three months later he's married? Think about it."

I thought about it. Bewildered, I said, "But, Parker, Mother and Daddy fell in love at first sight."

Parker spoke to me slowly, forcing himself to be patient. "Kelly, Dad would have married Ellen in a heartbeat. Mother was his second choice. And only because she was there. All this time, Mother has never felt sure that Dad really loves her."

"Ridiculous. He brings her presents every five minutes. She must have noticed by now."

"Okay, don't believe me. But there's no romance in those gifts, Kelly. He just has to keep shoveling this junk at her in order to keep her happy. She's a grown woman acting about fifteen. Wendy doesn't act like that," he finished contentedly. "I tell Wendy I love her, she believes me and that's that."

I resented his making Wendy sound better than Mom.

"Wendy and I," said Parker loftily, "have an honest relationship. No pretenses like Mom and Dad." He pranced off to his room, singing scraps of melody. Love songs to Wendy. I gathered up my quizzes. Lace, chocolate, laughter, candlelight, dancing . . . not romantic?

I rejected Parker's theory.

Because if my parents' romance was fake, then whose could be real?

Parker thought his with Wendy was real.

It had lasted three months.

But how long does love have to last to be real? If Daddy had loved Ellen for eight years and nothing came of it, then what *was* love anyhow?

Somebody made five hundred copies of my romance quizzes and passed them out in the halls the next day at school.

Public humiliation builds character, I told myself. I smiled when people teased. I agreed that *plaid* and *whipped cream* were pretty weird words on a romance quiz.

Parker pounced on me in the halls. Waving a quiz in his hand, he said furiously, "I cannot believe my own sister actually did this."

"It seemed reasonable at the time."

"Kelly, the whole school is—"

"I know, don't say it. Just stand next to me in a supportive fashion like a decent old big brother."

"It would be easier if you were a decent little sister. Do you know how people are laughing?"

"Yes, Park. I know."

He relented. Park hadn't been voted Nicest Boy for nothing. Putting an arm around me, a rare move for us, he said softly, "Good luck, Kelly. I think it's going to be a long week for you."

By the end of the day, however, teasing had tapered way

off. By the final class, not more than ten or twenty people even mentioned the quizzes.

I stole a look at Will.

He was not stealing one at me. He was listening to the American history teacher. How can anybody concentrate on the Last Frontier when there are important things happening, like the girl next to you being totally humiliated, needing a new compliment? One she can put on the shelf next to *You have the smile of a pixie*.

Wendy came on with her soap.

I relaxed, thinking it would take some of the heat off me.

"It's been a long sorrowful day for our beauteous Allegra," said Wendy. "Allegra"—Wendy's voice rose—"has taken"—Wendy's voice became frenzied, as if Allegra had taken an overdose or a flight to New Zealand—"a quiz on romance. Her score is forty-seven. She has failed miserably. The entire world knows now that Allegra is totally lacking in romantic appeal."

I stared at Will's back. How could he have done that? How could he possibly have told Wendy about my score?

"Taking to her bed," cried Wendy, "Allegra will eat nothing but classic SPAM. No whipped cream. No violins playing. In vain, Greg pounds upon her front door."

"Way to go, Kelly," said Honey.

Wendy played sound effects, stringed instruments and ratta-tap-tap of knuckles on wood.

I had sound effects of my own to endure. Laughter from every classroom at Cummington High. At me.

I put my head down on my arms and hid from my world. Which of them was worse—Will or Wendy? Bad enough that Will told. But my own brother's girlfriend using me like that? Turning me into material? Just the day before she had defended me and I had trusted her. She was definitely paying me back for riding in the backseat when she wanted to be alone with Parker.

Will's back remained motionless, broad and, in annoying coincidence, plaid. A wool plaid shirt I would gladly have strangled him with.

"Greg is not a man to glance backward," Wendy continued. "Jumping into his midnight blue car, Greg takes to the road. As he cruises past her house, the alluring Octavia, gowned in ruffles and velvet, redolent of lilac, rushes out into the street." Every time she used one of my words, she leaned into it and laughed slightly. "Greg slams on the brakes and shouts, 'Octavia! What is your romance quotient? Come! Take a test ride with me.'"

Faith said, "I think this is the best dialogue she's done in weeks."

Everybody else said, "Shhh!"

"But Octavia is beyond romance." Wendy's voice turned throaty. She rasped, "'Forget romance, Greg,' says Octavia. 'I'm pregnant.'"

There was no need to say "Shhh!" this time.

"'What I need is money,' says Octavia."

I don't suppose our teen pregnancy rate is different from the rest of the nation, but here in Cummington, we certainly don't refer to it. Teen sex, if indeed there is such a thing, occurs beyond the city limits.

In her bright wrap-up voice, Wendy continued, "Tune in tomorrow to find out if romance can—"

The mike went off.

There was time for everybody to notice that Octavia had not asked for marriage but for money. I could think of things she could do with Greg's money but regardless of her final selection, Octavia was not going to make Cummington happy.

Dr. Scheider read a few more announcements in a shaken voice.

Then the final bell rang and the class instead of leaving school burst into a discussion of the soap dialogue. They had forgotten my quiz. They talked about Octavia and Wendy.

When everybody was too caught up speculating about Wendy's future to be aware of him, Will turned around and held up his hand like a stop sign. "I didn't do it," he said fast.

I snarled at him.

"Really. I didn't tell her. Honest."

"Right. Wendy overheard us from the principal's office. Two floors and a half mile of hall from here."

"I don't blame you for suspecting me. Any detective would. But I'm innocent. It's coincidence. She picked forty-seven out of thin air."

"No air is that thin."

Will didn't give up. He was long enough to lean across the space between our desks, put both enormous hands on my books and look mournfully into my face. I considered smacking him but it would just draw more attention my way.

He was truly upset. I looked into the conceited eyes that had never bothered to focus on me and realized that Will Reed really wanted me to believe him. He cared about my opinion of him.

I could not understand. He had told Wendy—nobody else could have told her—and he could only have done it to be mean, so why care about me now?

"Could she have found your magazine?" asked Will. "Maybe you left it out and she and Park found it with your answers written in."

I *had* left the magazine in Park's car. Maybe she and Parker had taken the quiz. Jerk that I am, I had circled my answers. Wendy could add. Wendy would love adding up that she, Wendy Newcombe, was a Queen of Romance, and I, Kelly Williams, had failed the course.

I sighed and nodded. "Could be, Will. Okay. I believe you."

Will's anxiety faded. He smiled a real smile, a boy's smile, a warm and wide true smile at me.

For a moment as long as a crush, our eyes locked. My heart was pounding. I struggled to say or do something—anything!—to keep him looking at me like that. (Invite him over to make fudge? Throw a Frisbee? Ask to see his baby pictures?) But Will unfolded himself, reached his height of six feet four inches and loped silently out of the room.

At home, trauma was waiting.

My mother was holding a letter in her hand, staring at it as if it were a bomb. "What's wrong, Mom?" I said, frantic, thinking death, dismemberment, fatal disease, the relatives in Ohio. . . .

"Your father's high school reunion," said my mother bleakly. "He wants to go. He can't wait to go. I have to send in our acceptance."

"Oh, but, Mom! That'll be such fun. Even I can't wait for my high school reunion and I'm not even a senior. It'll be such fun to find out what happened to everybody. Whether they got what they hoped for. Whether our class had anybody famous in it. If the Most Likely to Succeed really did. Oooooh, Mom, you'll have a great time."

My mother flopped onto the couch and drooped all over the throw pillows.

"No, huh?" I said. "Why not?"

She shrugged, getting looser and floppier and more depressed all over the sofa. My brother's dumb lecture on Mother and Daddy's marriage came back to me. "Because of Ellen?" I said dubiously.

She leaped to her feet. "Kelly, what made you think of Ellen? Does Daddy talk about her? Why did you think of Ellen so quickly? How do you even know about Ellen? What is there to know?"

She was pale. She ran her tongue over her lips and I thought, Park was right! She's afraid of Ellen. "Because Daddy talks about her now and then when he's telling stories about when he was a boy," I said, trying to be casual. "That's all."

Mother shivered and sat down again.

"Oh, Mother, Ellen's probably fat and repulsive. Has five kids who are all delinquents. Thinks a big day is making instant chocolate pudding."

"No, she isn't." An involuntary shudder rippled over my mother's face and body. "Ellen already got her reunion invitation. She wrote to your father. She enclosed a photograph. She wants us to get together before the reunion."

"So what's she like? Can I see the photograph?"

My mother's smile was forced. "She's beautiful. Looks ten years younger than she is. And you can't see it. Your father has the letter and the photograph with him."

"With him? You don't mean in his wallet?"

"Maybe not in his wallet, but he didn't leave it behind."

I sat down next to her. For the first time in my life, she leaned on me. "I know how silly this is," she said. I felt like a woman friend, someone on her side, not her little girl. It felt wonderful, even though she was scaring me. "Ellen is stunning. She always was. And he was so excited to hear from her."

"Do you have the letter memorized? Quote it to me. I want to know what we're up against."

"Up against?" said my mother. "Kelly, I've felt up against Ellen for a long time. If I gain five pounds, I know Ellen would never lose her figure. If I forget the punch line to a joke, I know Ellen would tell more sophisticated jokes and never forget the ending. If I get lazy for a few weeks, I know Ellen has endless energy and everything she does is brilliant and makes money and headlines."

I giggled. "I feel that way about half my class."

The doors were flung open. In came Wendy and Parker.

Mother ceased to be a woman friend and became a mom after school, offering Oreo cookies and ginger ale while the children chattered. Passing out napkins. Listening.

"So you got suspended for two days," said Parker to Wendy. "It's not the end of the world."

"It is the end. I don't like to be in trouble. I just like to make a splash."

At my expense, I thought. I willed Wendy to look sorry and guilty the way Will had, but she didn't notice. It was so ordinary for her to use people that she forgot in the space of a few hours she'd ever done it.

I was still envious of Wendy. I'd always be envious of Wendy. But I no longer wanted to be Wendy.

Maybe she dates Parker because subconsciously she

wants his niceness to rub off on her, I thought. Maybe she's attracted to the one thing she doesn't have.

Wendy split her Oreos, licked the icing off and set the uneaten chocolate halves back on the table. Now, there's self-control.

Parker told Mom about the soap opera dialogue and how Dr. Scheider felt that since a possible use for that money was abortion or becoming a single mother, Wendy had to think more clearly about the effect of her soap opera on her innocent listeners, and therefore the best deterrence to future unpleasant dialogue was suspension. I thought dismemberment would be better but I restrained myself from saying so. I would have had to admit that I was the one with the forty-seven intimacy quotient.

"Well," said my mother, "the school doesn't like you to pretend that pregnancy can happen to high school juniors."

Wendy and Parker and I were for once united. "Pretend?" we said.

Mother shuddered. "I prefer to believe that."

"You're wrong. You're an ostrich with your head in the sand," Parker said.

"I like having my head in the sand. I don't want details. Always avoid details," she instructed us. She ate an Oreo cookie to distract herself.

"A good parent," said Parker, "is supposed to be on the watch for clues that her children—"

"Hush. Now, Wendy. You call your mother so she won't think you're running away from this."

"Look who's talking," said Parker. "You're the one running away, Mom."

She ignored him and dialed Wendy's home number for her, handing over the phone. There is one thing Mom can't run away from, I thought. And that is Dad's reunion and Ellen being there.

It seemed that Wendy's mother had already heard from Dr. Scheider. He was probably regretting his call. Mrs. Newcombe had given him a sharp lecture on civil liberties, freedom of speech, the use of school air time and the pregnancy rate at Cummington High.

Dr. Scheider decided he had been hasty giving a suspension to Wendy and of course he no longer meant it and yes Wendy could go on the air again tomorrow. Although he did insist that Octavia's pregnancy had to end.

Parker had suggestions for how Wendy could end Octavia's pregnancy. Mother made him stop. Wendy said, "You know, not to be rude, Mrs. Williams, but you are kind of an ostrich with your head in the sand."

"Go eat Oreos," said my mother, and Parker and Wendy left the kitchen.

I waited to see if Mom would bring up Ellen again, but she got out a cake mix and the bowls and beaters. I love cake mixes. No effort and a minute later you have a bowl to lick. You could buy the cake at the grocery store bakery with even less effort, but you wouldn't have the bowl to lick. I think it's too bad you have to bake the cake. I like to have batter raw. Once I had a whole cup of batter.

But Mom put everything back in the cupboards without making anything. "No more desserts," she mumbled. "I have to lose ten pounds."

"Why?"

"I have to look good at his reunion."

I would have laughed except she was serious.

"You should have seen how your father held that photograph," she said, leaning on the counter, as if the shelf where the mixer sat were too high to reach ever again. "He handled it like gold. Like precious—" She broke off.

Our conversation did not continue. Mom fled to her room, which I do constantly but had never seen her do.

I went on up to my room too, and opened my romance game board. I wanted to be on the Start Heart with Will. I wanted Mom and Dad to be at Happily Ever After where they belonged. I wanted—

"Kelly! Telephone!" shouted Parker. He was irked. I understood. All phone calls should always be for you. No fair running to get the phone and it's for somebody else. Since Park and I each have our own phone, it's unusual for us to get calls on the family line. It would not be Faith, which was okay with me, because I wasn't sure how much of the day's dialogue I wanted to discuss even with her.

"Hello?" I said.

"Kelly?"

It was Will. I recognized his voice instantly, just from the two syllables of my name. Will calling me up! I had to lie down. "Hi, Will. How are you?"

"Did you know my voice or do you have caller ID?"

"I knew your voice. You and I chatter so much, remember, disrupting every class."

Will laughed. He knew we'd had about two exchanges during our entire lifetimes. "Well, I guess Wendy rescued you," he said. "She didn't mean to, but everybody's already forgotten your romance quiz and they're talking exclusively about Octavia being pregnant and Wendy getting suspended."

"You make Octavia sound real."

"She is real. We know more about what Octavia's doing than our own families. I was wondering if you're going to kill Wendy or not."

"I considered it. But Parker wouldn't like it."

"Why does he go out with her anyway?" said Will distastefully.

I was so struck by that. Everybody else wondered why Wendy went out with Parker. Only Will wondered why Parker went out with Wendy.

"I thought I'd tell you my intimacy quotient," said Will.

"I've been worried," I admitted. "Did you do better than me? Are you capable of tons of intimacy or do you need counseling?"

"I got ninety-three. My social life is what everybody else aspires to."

"Maybe *you* should go out with Wendy," I said. "You could stack your conceit next to hers any day."

Will laughed. "Actually I made that score up. The quiz

was so dumb I didn't bother to answer the questions. How can you stand stuff like that? It doesn't have anything to do with real-life romance."

But I don't have any real-life romance, I thought. I have to make do with whatever the magazines offer.

I turned the phone over in my hand. It was so much larger than my cell phone, as if it were full of possible conversations, like my heart. Ask me out, Will. Give me real-life romance so that I don't have to renew my magazine subscriptions.

"Actually," said Will, very casually, "I have to go to this dinner-dance, because I'm an All-State player and I have to be at this honor dinner."

A few weeks before, I had disliked Will.

Now I stared down at my board game, still open. My handsome boys, all nines and tens on a scale of attractiveness. There was Will, covering up Oriental Avenue. In real life, I thought, there would be sixes and threes and zeroes as well. There would be stars and losers, people hard to notice and people barely there. But who wants real life? In the game of romance, don't you always want the stars?

I jerked my mind off the game. I was out of the game league. I was listening to the start of the real thing. My first date with anybody at all on earth would be an important dinner-dance with Will. I clung to the phone.

"And what I want to ask is," said Will, taking an exceptionally deep breath, "since you're such a close friend of

Megan, and I don't know if she's still going out with Jimmy or not, can you tell me what her situation is right now before I call her?"

I truly felt as if the ceiling had lowered. It was pressing me down onto my bed, laughing at me, squashing my hopes, my pride and my body. Life was indeed a game, and such fun, too.

"They've split for good," I said.

"Oh," said Will, pleased. "Thanks, Kelly."

So what about the pixie smile? I thought. Is Megan's smile pixier? Or is *pixie* an insult, and not a compliment? "Why did you bring up the romance quiz, Will? You want my opinion on what's romantic for your honor dinner with Megan?" And then I didn't give him time to answer, but started sniping at him, the kind of conversation Honey always has—half nasty. I hated myself. I wanted to say sweet things, good things. But Will wanted to say those things to Megan.

At last we managed to say good-bye.

To keep from crying, which I told myself the situation did not deserve, I sketched board game cartoons. I had Jimmy walking the squares with Megan. Jimmy gaining a bowling partner. Jimmy tossing Megan to the sidelines. Will rolling a double and heading for Megan. Faith rushing headlong around the curves. Parker and Wendy three squares away from Happily Ever After. Jeep losing a turn.

Suppose you were dealt a hand. Suppose you had a deck

of fifty-two guys. Suppose some were great and some got mixed reviews and some made you throw up.

LANCE	tall	football franchise owner	sexy	cute
BART	short	unemployed	stingy	good dancer
JOEL	fat	attorney	generous	funny
KEVIN	skinny	bus driver	owns no toothbrush	great hair

Okay. You dealt out these cards. Then what? Trade them with other players? Run into roadblocks where you had to surrender one and gain another? Have a card of your own where you had to impress the boy cards so they'd stay?

How awful. How much like life.

I wanted the romance game to be fun and I wanted you always to win. Why play a game if you're going to lose? Especially if it's the game of romance?

I stared at my game half the evening because it was better than weeping over Will. Actually I would not have wept over Will, because I still didn't really like him. I would have wept over me, because nobody loved me.

Around midnight, Parker came home.

Since we had school the next day, he was in trouble. Dad was waiting up for him. I braced for shouting, but there wasn't any. Quiet talking at the foot of the stairs and then Dad's voice, soft as a pat. "Try to get some sleep. It'll be better in the morning."

Better in the morning? A car accident, maybe?

"Oh, right," said Parker sarcastically. He came heavily up the stairs. I pretended to be getting a glass of water so I could bump into him in the hall. "Wow, Park. Where were you and Wendy, midnight on a school night?"

My brother stopped in the narrow hall. His ski jacket rubbed against the wallpaper with a slick whispery sound. The night-light near our knees threw shadows over his features. His eyes were pools of dark and his hair seemed longer, his shoulders wider. When he spoke, his voice was like lead.

"We broke up. Wendy went back to Jeep."

CHAPTER

Where is the fun in a game that leaves one of the players devastated?

Wendy, presumably, was off having a wonderful time with Jeep. And Jeep, who had wanted her back so much, was undoubtedly having a wonderful time with Wendy.

But Parker could not eat, would not speak, did not concentrate and stayed off the phone.

Mom made Park his favorite meals. Dad volunteered to take Park to an ice hockey game at the Coliseum. Parker ignored them or glanced briefly in their direction as if they were crazy. Perhaps they were.

Whatever Parker had felt for Wendy, it was too deep to be assuaged by a pair of tickets to a hockey game. I could actually see my brother ache. Seventeen, and his joints were stiff and he moved slowly and unwillingly. When any of our phones rang, but especially his own, he'd stiffen and look at the phone as if it were the enemy, but with the potential of being his closest friend. His Wendy.

But Wendy never called.

Did she ever love him? I wondered. What is love, anyhow?

How can Parker have had so much of it and now it's simply gone? Is love an electric current? Throw a switch and it flows elsewhere? While the other love vanishes like a burned-out bulb?

My own thoughts were filled with Will. I had never thought so intensely about a boy at all, never mind a boy I didn't like. What had he ever done that was appealing or friendly or kind or any of the things he himself had listed under love? At last I admitted the truth. I had a crush on Will.

Why? I thought despairingly. Why on the boy who calls me up to discuss another girl?

Angie did not ask Faith out.

Faith should have known. I think she did know. It was just unbearable to contemplate—being rejected. Both she and Parker were walking wounded. Parker bled internally and never talked, but Faith talked endlessly. I never told her about Will. There was nothing to tell. And yet my emotions were incredibly strong and totally private.

In sociology, Wendy was her usual bubbly self.

"How could she go out with Park for three months," I whispered to Faith, "and it doesn't show? There's nothing left of it?"

"It's as if they wrote that love in the sand at low tide," said Faith, "and the waves wiped it away, leaving no record."

Wendy continued to write her soap operas. They continued to be funny. Whatever happened to Octavia was not announced over the public-address system. School jokes about possible endings were told for days, however, and Wendy thrived on the attention. She wrote her dialogue exclusively during sociology now, passing the scripts over to Jeep for his approval. Jeep always told her that that day's soap was the best ever.

At home, the game of romance now included history.

"For God's sake, Violet!" shouted my father one night at dinner. "It's nothing but a meal. Three hundred people having overcooked roast beef or underdone salmon and telling each other we don't look any different. That's all the reunion will be."

"I understand, George. I understand perfectly."

"Good. Ellen is in the past, that's all. We'll have this one dinner the following night with her husband what's-his-name and that's it."

My mother stared into her water glass and whirled it until the ice cubes tinkled against each other.

"Ellen was always a very kind and understanding person," said my father.

"Oh? Am I going to require extra kindness and understanding?"

"Violet! Ellen will be an excellent hostess. You'll love her."

"You mean you'll love her."

"I do not love Ellen."

"Then why do you keep bringing her up?"

A week of this and we were all ready to shoot somebody. It was just that nobody could agree who deserved to be shot. Ellen for existing? Mom for overreacting? Dad for losing his temper and stomping off?

"See what I mean?" Parker said to me. "See how ridiculous this is? Mom is weak. Dad is dumb."

"That's not true," I said, although it appeared to be.

"I don't know what Mom thinks is going to happen," muttered Park. "Does she think old Ellen is going to snatch Dad away from her? That Ellen will divorce what's-his-name and Dad will divorce Mom?"

It terrified me. "I suppose that could happen." If it did, I would definitely find that counselor. Forget my intimacy quotient. I would never survive my parents' divorce.

"It could not happen," said Parker sharply.

"You had faith in Wendy and look what happened when the competition showed up."

Parker did not argue. He just faded. The lines in his face deepened until he could have been Dad's age.

"What did happen, anyway?" I asked. I hated not knowing. Not only did it mean I couldn't answer when the entire school asked me about Park and Wendy, it meant I couldn't help Park either.

My brother's answer was the last I could ever have expected.

"I yelled at her for mocking you," he told me.

"But—but you were so worried about *her* when we sat in the kitchen with Mom. You didn't say one word about her using me."

"I didn't know then. She told me later when we went out. She said she found your quiz in the magazine and saw your score written in the margin and decided to use it."

"You defended me?" I said slowly. I thought, His love life ended because he was his usual nice self. And about his dumb little sister who's always a pain when he has a chance to use the car.

"She picked a fight. It was like she wanted a fight so she could storm off and go back to Jeep. I felt like we were following one of her scripts. She was laughing at you. She said you were a—" Parker stopped, didn't say whatever word Wendy had used and went on. "I got furious and yelled at her, which I have never done, and she took out her cell phone and right there in front of me called Jeep to come and rescue her."

I could not even picture this. How absolutely horrible for Park. He had sat there in his own car while Wendy changed drivers. Had Jeep demanded to know why Wendy needed rescue? Had Jeep said, What, you're hurting her? You some monster or something?

We were sitting on my bed. Park was slumped against the headboard.

"Oh, Park." I felt sick for him. "You'll find somebody else, though," I said cheerily. "Don't worry too much."

What a jerk I sounded like.

I loved my brother for standing up for me, and yet if this was the result, he should have laughed with Wendy. But he was nice. He wouldn't laugh at anybody, even me.

"I don't want somebody else." The despair in his voice matched the lines on his face.

It's better to have played the game and lost, I thought, than to be like me, not playing at all. Nobody's voice had ever sunk in despair because of me and I had never felt despair over anybody either. At least Park could feel pain.

I tried to explain that.

"Kelly," said my brother, "that's like telling a cancer victim that now that he's dying, he can appreciate life. It's stupid. I don't want to be a better, stronger person because of this. I want to be plain old me with Wendy at my side."

When Parker went into his room, I sat on my bed to stare at my romance board. Currently it featured a great heart with three paths: pink, pale pink and white. You went around the heart three times and ended up in the center, resting on Cupid's arrow. Little cherubs danced around and wedding bouquets fell into your final square. I'd spent a lot of money on rubber stamps with exactly the right pictures and I was artistically delighted with the result.

The paths were divided into squares. Each was a Good Thing. Nice dates, sunny weather, sleek cars, lovely gifts, strong hugs, passionate kisses. I'd had such fun making up the dates. I'd never written so many exclamation points in my life.

A picnic by the sea! Sunburned but happy!

A bicycle built for two! Windblown and in love!

You two go hang gliding! In heaven with a heavenly boy!

But in our house, my brother was devastated, my mother terrified, my father furious, and I was simply lonely.

How pitiful the game was. In real life, nobody deals you a perfect anything, let alone rows of delightful boyfriends. And to spend every day, every square, doing a Good Thing with this splendid person?

I kicked the board game under my bed to get it out of our lives.

CHAPTER

“No,” said Megan. “Absolutely not, Mrs. Williams. Since you’re asking, I will tell you. That outfit is wrong, wrong, wrong, wrong, wrong.”

My mother looked longingly into my full-length mirror.

“You have become invisible,” Megan told her. “You are wearing a skin-toned dress. Flesh-colored makeup. Clear nail polish. You can’t seriously want to wear this to the reunion.”

“Of course I can. And there’s nothing wrong with this outfit or being invisible,” said my mother.

“Then you’re a success,” Megan told her. “People won’t be able to shake hands with you because they won’t be able to find your hand against that dress.”

My mother was no match for anyone in those clothes. It was odd how I too had come to think of Ellen as competition to be fought down. I wanted my mother to win easily. We ought to have one winner in the family at least.

"Go put on that purple dress," said Megan firmly. "Really. No kidding, it's perfect. The saleswoman who talked you into buying it had excellent taste and was right. Put it on and then we'll accessorize you." Megan turned to me. "God knows, after all these years of gifts from your father, she must have more accessories than the department store anyway."

"But not many that go with purple," said my mother.

"Yes, you do," I told her. "You have at least a billion violet things."

"Violet is not purple. Violet is sweet dark lavender. That dress I paid a small fortune for is as purple as strobe lights." Mother heaved a huge deep sigh and slunk back to her room to try it on.

"I had no idea high school reunions were so scary," Megan said to me. "Especially when it isn't even her reunion."

I did not explain Fear of Ellen and how it ranked in our family. I did not want that problem to become Fox Meadow property. "Mom thinks she'll be on display and she's nervous. Now go back to telling me about Will. You actually turned him down?"

Megan gloated. "Yes. I loved turning him down. I felt so good afterward."

I lay back on my bed. In the next room I could hear

Mother rustling, slithering out of one dress into the next. I could feel the many seams of the patchwork denim spread making lines on my skin. I could feel myself inside my clothes. But I could not feel what Megan was feeling.

"Power," explained Megan. "Jimmy had such power over me. He could ruin my schedule, reduce me to tears, leave me feeling foolish and ugly and unloved."

"But that was Jimmy. This is Will."

"You don't understand," said Megan. Which was certainly true. "Jimmy likes that drippy little bowling freak better than he likes me. Did you take a look at her? A loser. It's worse losing out to a loser than to a winner." Megan made a series of terrible faces and admired each expression in my mirror.

Perhaps Ellen felt that way. Perhaps now she thought she'd been wrong to leave my father. Did she wonder how Dad could choose Mother after beautiful brilliant Ellen? Perhaps Ellen felt that Dad had married a loser.

"I've never been dumped before," confided Megan, "and I plan never to be dumped again. I'll always be the dumper, not the dump-ee."

"You mean," I said slowly, "that you said no to Will because it made you feel better about Jimmy?"

Megan nodded. "Ooooh, great nail polish," she said, landing on the gift boxes Faith was always raiding. "I saw this advertised and I meant to get it for myself. May I try it, Kelly? Thanks." She unscrewed the top and began stroking color over her nails.

Poor Will, I thought. He had no importance to Megan. She didn't even turn him down because of him. He wasn't even worth turning down. She turned him down because of Jimmy, and Will will never know that. He'll wonder if it was his breath or his personality, his bony face or his smelly feet. (Actually I don't know if his feet smell. I never had the opportunity, if that's what you'd call it, to find out; it was just an example.)

My mother came back into the room wearing another old dress, and not her new one, and Megan glanced over and said, "No! Mrs. Williams. That color is vomit green and the style is for old women when they're weeding in their gardens. You should not even have it in your house.

"Anyway, Mrs. Williams, don't be mad at me for saying this, but it makes you look fat," added Megan, dealing the ultimate slam on the green dress. "Other people at the reunion will be thin."

My mother cringed.

Megan rammed her point home. "They'll lord it over you if you look fat."

"I'm dieting," said my mother desperately. "Really. I'm down two pounds."

If there is a God, I thought, he could make Ellen gain weight between now and the reunion. Develop a craving for cream-filled doughnuts so she has to show up in size forty-four polyester pants.

But Ellen was the kind who would never get fat. I knew

from her yearbook picture. She would always manage to be superior to the rest of us. The way Megan was superior to me.

Megan was helping with Mother's clothes, but she wasn't doing it to be helpful. She was showing my mother that she, at sixteen, knew more about style than Mother ever would. She was enjoying every minute of being the expert with the beginner.

Do I even like Megan? I thought. She's my lifelong friend and now I'm not sure I like her. I don't like how she treated Will and I don't like how she's treating Mom.

I thought about how Daddy was treating Mother. He had stopped bringing presents and cards. I thought he was annoyed over the whole Ellen behavior but Mom thought it was proof that his dreams were about Ellen.

Over Ellen, who lived two thousand miles away, they were going to break down.

What terrible timing it all was.

Perhaps what my board game needed was an element of timing. Good timing and bad. Things that came together by accident as well as by planning. Things that would fall apart when nobody wanted them to and things that would never have an explanation.

Mother came in wearing the purple dress.

"Yes!" shouted Megan, clapping. "It's you. Streamlined, but feminine. Flared romantic hemline and just a speck sexy at the neck. I love how that fabric falls. And it's your color. Utterly. Yes. Excellent!"

I liked Megan again. My mother was smiling. Nervously, but smiling.

"You'll make a real splash, Mom," I told her. "I love it."

Mother looked hopeful.

"Now you need a really good necklace," said Megan authoritatively. "Something that makes a statement."

Mother looked helpless.

"That enormous silver violet on the silver rope Daddy gave you years ago," I suggested. "The one you thought was too big to wear and you let me wear it on Halloween when I was a Gypsy."

My mother made a face. "It's way too large."

"Not with this dress."

"I think I don't have it anymore," said my mother hopefully.

"Forget it. I know just where it is." I raced to my parents' bedroom. All Fox Meadow houses have walk-in closets—two per master bedroom. Mother's flows over into Daddy's and she keeps the presents she doesn't know what to do with in their gift boxes tucked in the corners. Megan went with me because she loves to snoop. "When is the reunion?" she wanted to know. "Tomorrow?"

"Of course not. It's a whole month away. In this household we like to leave lots of time for panicking." I unearthed a vast silver violet.

"Ouch," said Megan. "Well, let's try it."

We went back and draped it around Mom's neck. "It is large," admitted Megan, "but the effect is awesome. Wear it. Well, I have to run. Places to go, boys to see." She smiled brilliantly and raced out of the room, narrowly missing Parker coming up. The house was a thoroughfare.

"I wish I had someplace to go that made me so happy," said Park, glancing after Megan. "Listen, Mom, do we have anything good to eat in this house?"

"Yes. And if you'll eat every bit of it, then I won't. Deal?"

"Deal. Awesome dress, Mom," said Park.

I was stunned. Wendy had accomplished something worthy. Parker was aware of women's clothing and knew enough to say so. Way to go, Wendy.

They went downstairs companionably while I fished out my board game and the boy cards I'd crunched up and thrown in the wastebasket. Nothing was wrinkled beyond repair. I got out my iron and ironed the papers, which worked quite well. Then I erased every fourth or fifth Good Thing on the board and stuck in terrible, painful, agonizing, inexplicable stuff instead. That was much easier to think up than Good Things.

I erased *Sunshine*. I wrote: *He never calls; you never know why. Lose one turn.*

I erased a *Delirium of Love* square. I wrote *Abandonment.*

I got rid of *Crazy with Happiness* and tossed in *Depression.* Then I replaced *Depression* with *Melancholia.* That sounded *really* depressed.

The phone rang.

I picked it up absently.

"Hi, Kelly. It's Will."

If I was surprised the first time, I was astounded the second time. "Hi, Will."

"You do your sociology yet?" he asked.

"I breezed through the chapter. It was the English assignment that killed me. William Faulkner. I haven't understood a word since page one but somehow I've arrived at page seventy-three."

That was my stable marriage score, I thought. It's got to be significant.

"That's a lot to plow through," said Will. "We've been spared Faulkner in my English class." He began discussing a particular law of physics that was giving him problems for an upcoming exam.

"And what about Megan turning you down?" I said, before I thought.

Oh, what's the matter with tongues? Why aren't they securely latched to minds? Now he'd know that we had gossiped about it and that Megan had told everybody.

Into the silent phone I babbled, "It was mean of her, Will, but it didn't have anything to do with you. It was about Jimmy. She's still mad at him for dumping her. It made her feel good to take it out on a boy. Any boy."

The silence continued.

I had run out of babble.

Will said, "I think you are the first girl I've ever run into who says things honestly. Truth and all that. You are remarkable, Kelly."

Forget remarkable, I thought. Tell me sexy and beautiful.

We began talking. For almost an hour we talked. We covered girls, dates, Megan, Jimmy, truth, lies, Ms. Simms, Wendy's soap. I loved it. I could have talked all night. The more Will talked, the more I liked him. The less conceited he sounded. The more my crush came back.

Do I want it back? I thought.

Do I have any choice? I thought five minutes later.

"It's pretty late," said Will finally. "And I haven't actually started my homework yet. I'd better go."

"Oh. I'm sorry. I had more to say."

"Me too. See you tomorrow, Kelly. Thanks for listening."

I held my cell phone after he hung up as if he were still part of it, as if the little black oblong contained some of him and some of me. Then I went into my bathroom to look at myself in strong light and see if there was a girl in the mirror whom Will Reed could have a crush on.

There were two ways to read "See you tomorrow, Kelly."

One: We shared fourth and sixth periods and at some point his eyes would naturally focus in my direction and he would see me.

Two: He could hardly wait for the next day to come so he could see me, Kelly Williams, good listener.

I wasn't sure I liked that closing line of Will's. "Thanks for listening" sounded sisterly. I had friends; I was a sister. I wanted dates.

I wandered back to my room to find Parker lying on my bed, holding my board game over his head, reading the squares and laughing like a maniac.

"You rotten worthless brother. You spy. Get up off my bed. Stop reading that. Stop laughing at me. That's private, Parker. I hate you."

Parker merely swung the game out of my reach and kept laughing. "Kelly, the game is terrific. It's so funny. I love it."

I didn't want it to be funny. I wanted it to show the sweet side and the bleak side of romance.

"But, Kell," he said, sitting up and crossing his ankles and spreading the game before him, "you've designed it so that only girls can play. Revise it. Make it so boys can play as well. Girl cards and girl pronouns and girl names as well as boy names and stuff."

"How can I do that? That's too hard. Anyway, name me a single boy on the face of the earth who would be caught playing The Game of Romance."

Parker ignored this. "Your sentences read *He loves you* and *He brings you flowers*. Change those to *Your date loves you. Your date brings you flowers*."

It wouldn't take much except to erase. I could even redo the game on fresh paper.

"*He takes you to Europe*," read Parker. "*He brings you a dozen red roses. He teaches you to water-ski*." Parker frowned. "You're sexist, making the boy do everything."

"I am not sexist. This is my game. For me. What am I supposed to put—*He or she brings you a dozen red roses?*"

Parker began erasing. He put *Your date brings you*. He was a very careful eraser. As he erased, I rewrote. It was kind of pleasant to be a team.

"Furthermore," said Parker, "exactly how old and exactly how rich are these dates of yours? Instead of skiing in Switzerland or a cruise in the Caribbean you should share milk shakes or go bowling."

Eraser specks flew. He took out really good ones like *Explore a coral reef together in your new scuba equipment* and wrote *You run into each other at the delicatessen.*

"Now we need some really crummy boring rotten dates," said Park, warming up like a baseball pitcher and getting mean.

I watched him add crummy boring rotten dates.

"I don't want that much reality," I protested. "This is a romance game. The way you're setting it up, a person could have a flat tire and the dog gets carsick and you miss the movie and you lose your credit cards and then the person you love moves away and never writes. What's romantic about that?"

Parker just blew eraser specks away. They dusted my face.

"Park?" I said. "Do you think Wendy planned to break up with you? Was she just waiting for the moment she could blame the end of your romance on you? So she could script it the way she wanted it? Rescue by Jeep from the clutches of Park?"

Park erased quite a few squares we hadn't discussed yet. I memorized them as they vanished so I could write them back in later.

Parker straightened up, stretched his legs, tucked them back and began sorting through my boy cards. "These are good," he said in surprise. "Here you've got reality. Some boys are funny, some are fat. Some are rich and some have eight hundred zits." He read each card slowly.

I really ought to have the opinions of boys on my boy cards, I thought.

I could not quite imagine myself inviting Will and Jeep and Angie over to study my romance game and give me a few hints.

"When she was leaving with Jeep," said Park, "Wendy told me it was all an act. She never loved me. She kept tapping me with her purse instead of touching me with her hands."

Wendy carried a teeny lime green purse, square, on a long thin leather loop. The purse had exactly enough room for her driver's license and some cash. Her cell phone fit into a little pocket on the exterior and her pencils and pens she clipped to her notebook. Faith said once that there wasn't room in that purse for Tampax. We decided Wendy didn't have periods. They weren't romantic enough.

I could just see Wendy giving Parker little miniature bruises with her little miniature purse. But the bruises were enormous and real.

"Her voice breaking on the phone with you?" I said. "Her hugging you and leaning on your shoulder? An act? I think we should go after her with a shotgun. Queen of Romance? Parker, she was Queen Bitch."

The poster slid off the bed and landed softly on my carpet, the huge hearts sideways, and then it flipped over so the hearts were hidden.

"Don't say things like that," said my brother.

He still loves her, I thought. She could be a rabid dog and he would still love her. How awful love is. Or how awful Wendy is.

I put my arm around Park.

Not all love is romantic. Some is brother/sister love.

Love is also comfort.

CHAPTER

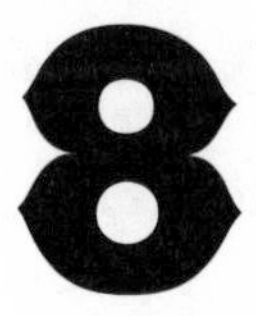

I was sound asleep on top of the covers. School had exhausted me. I had not even undressed, but was sprawled over my homework and had a pencil poking me in the side. I answered the phone groggily.

"This is important," said Megan. "You're going to get a call at ten o'clock, Kelly, and you and I have to sort out the details so you don't screw up. Do you remember Blaize?"

Nobody named Blaize came to mind.

"I dated him in eighth grade," said Megan, as one referring to ancient civilization. "He's from Prospect Hill. There's a big dance Saturday night and his girlfriend broke up with him and he called and asked me to go with him but I can't—I'm far too busy—so I gave him your number. I promised Blaize that you are good company, a great date, pretty, slender, interested in sports."

"I'm slender, anyway."

"Do you have a formal gown or do you need to borrow one of mine?" Megan sounded so crisp. Perhaps she had a checklist in front of her. Steps to Take When Fixing Up Your Friend with Blaize.

"I need to borrow one of yours," I admitted. Megan has been to so many formal dances, she has a wardrobe of gowns the way I have a wardrobe of T-shirts.

"Fine. Tomorrow after school we'll do the dress part. Now. On this date. Be sure to joke a lot. He's a bad dancer, so don't force him to dance. Be very relaxed. He's into sports but he didn't make varsity in basketball so don't mention basketball." Megan went on and on. I was dazed. How could I be relaxed when I had to memorize a forty-point checklist?

"Blaize is good stuff, Kelly. You don't want to mess up."

My hands were sweaty and my cheeks were feverish and I hadn't even talked to Blaize yet. I promised Megan that I would be slender, pretty, interested in sports (except basketball) and full of jokes.

A person needs a snack to consider this kind of thing. I headed for the kitchen and was immediately joined by Mom in her robe and Parker in his pajama bottoms. The sound of one person opening the refrigerator always brings the rest of us.

"What did Megan want?" said Mom.

"She's fixing me up with her old friend Blaize, who needs a Saturday night formal dance date because his girlfriend walked out on him."

"Perfect for your romance game!" cried my mother. "Can't you see a whole life together built on the coincidence of Blaize's girlfriend dumping him and you appearing in his life that very week?"

It sounded pretty darn similar to the coincidence of Ellen, Dad and Mom. "How do you know about my board game?" I said.

"I vacuum in there. You leave it out."

"You snoop," I said indignantly.

"She isn't a snoop, Kelly," said Parker. "You're messy. And there is nothing romantic about the dance. This poor guy Blaize gets dumped. He feels lower than low. He calls the only other girl he can think of and what does Megan do? Passes him on to a stranger like a helping of mashed potatoes at the table. What's so romantic about that?"

"It has romantic potential," said my mother stiffly.

"Romance is a crock," said Parker.

The clock chimed ten and my phone rang. "He's punctual, anyway," I said to them. I left them in the kitchen and tore back up the stairs so I could talk in the privacy of my room. "Hello?"

"Kelly there?"

"This is Kelly."

He said nothing more.

"Really," I said, remembering the instruction to joke a lot. "It's true. This is Kelly."

He forced a laugh. "And this is Blaize Devaney. Did—um—Megan—um—?"

I was thinking of Will. Would it ever occur to Will to ask me out? Would going someplace with this complete stranger jeopardize that? But of course, Will would never know I was going anywhere with Blaize because Blaize was from Prospect Hill. "Yes," I said. "Megan called." Am I insane? I thought. Worrying whether I should stay loyal to Will? Will, who would rank me one on a scale of one hundred? What is my problem? "And I'd love to go to the dance with you, Blaize."

"Oh. Great. Well." His voice sounded as if it came from a corpse. "Thanks for bailing me out," he said finally.

"You're welcome." I struggled to think of something amusing but failed and gave him driving directions to my house instead. Maybe it was a bad sign that Megan had been too busy for this guy. With whom was she so busy? Not Jimmy. Not Will. Not me or Faith.

"I'll pick you up at eight," he said, and we hung up.

I scooped up my board game. I put my finger on the Start Heart and slid myself slowly over the lacy pink line into the first square. "Romance," I told myself. "You asked for it, you got it, Kelly."

All week, the dialogue repeated itself.

"I love romance." That was Mother, of course.

"Poor Blaize." That was Parker.

"My little girl, starting to get flowers from guys." That was Dad, listing possibilities for the corsage Blaize would surely bring. "Carnations, orchids, roses, baby's breath. I can see them all out there, a whole greenhouse, coming your way, Kelly." He was proud of me, as if he'd done something special, bringing up his daughter to swoon over flowers.

My mother wore a peculiar expression. All of a sudden I didn't want those flowers after all. I didn't want to be like Mother, not feeling loved unless little gifts littered my life to prove it. I wanted love that was kindness and forgiveness and laughter and—and all the other things Will had said.

I wanted to call Will up and tell him about my parents' marriage. The most romantic marriage in Cummington, frail enough that a weekend one month away was tearing it apart. A marriage whose cement was Hallmark cards and silver violets.

Marriage, maybe, that had lasted eighteen years on romance, and not on love?

My hair is slippery. Other girls with long hair can put it up in little braids and twists and interesting details. Mine just slides out and slithers down my cheek and neck. Clips and barrettes and scrunchies cascade to the floor and my hair is back where it started, flat, shiny and smooth, as if it had never been disturbed.

"It's like a law of nature," said my mother, struggling to do something unique with it. "It never allows anything to interrupt its chosen path."

"Stop worrying," advised Parker. "All Blaize needs is a presentable female body walking in the door with him."

It was Daddy who brought me a present: a gold charm to slip on my necklace. It wouldn't show because of the way the neckline of Megan's dress was cut, but that didn't matter. The charm was a tiny delicate eighth note. "Because tonight is music," said my father, who was happier about my date with Blaize than anybody, including me. "A prelude of things to come."

He sounded like a line off a greeting card. Were his gifts to Mom, his attentions to her, just a curtain to stand behind? Was he simply lubricating life so all things would slide his way? And now Mother was demanding more: love and reassurance instead of plain old romance? And he did not have that to give?

"Park," said Dad, "you sound as if you could use a presentable female body of your own."

"Yeah, well, I don't have an important affair on Saturday where I have to appear in public."

"You have a senior prom," I pointed out.

"Months away."

"It's not that far off, Park," said my mother. "My goodness, I wasn't thinking. How the calendar flies by. You'll have to put Wendy out of your mind and start dating other girls."

"If Park can put Wendy out of his mind," said my father, "how about you put Ellen out of your mind?"

We stood there, my family and I, and Ellen was in there with us, and a million bouquets that meant nothing, and a future that frightened us all. I couldn't see my parents clearly. Dad seemed angry and menacing. Mother shrank and turned wispy. Parker reduced himself to a shadow so he wouldn't have to participate.

Talk about it, I prayed. Talk about how dumb this is. Admit that Ellen doesn't matter. We matter. We, the Williams family. Say you love each other.

But nobody said anything.

The doorbell rang. My father went downstairs to let Blaize in and Parker followed to take a look at Blaize. Mother began folding things strewn around my room. She likes to fold. Make order out of chaos.

So make some order out of your own chaos, I thought. What is a sweatshirt on the floor compared to a marriage in shambles?

"Kelly, come on down," said my father loudly, with such gusto that he sounded like a quiz show emcee.

I swallowed, shivered and went down.

Blaize was very, very handsome. Megan was too busy to go out with this? He intimidated me just standing there. Just existing in all his male beauty. My steps faltered halfway down the stairs.

"What a great dress!" exclaimed Blaize.

I relaxed. One compliment and I had my act together again. So this is why Mom needs compliments, I thought. You feel so much better. You feel so much more in control when somebody tells you that you look good.

Blaize, smiling, took a half step toward me.

My mind moved at the speed of light, whipping through the next several years. I took Blaize through dating, being seniors together, going to both of our senior proms, attending the same college and getting married.

I wasn't even at the bottom of the stairs yet.

"Kelly," he said, greeting me, but also confirming that he liked what he saw. If there was a test, I had passed his, and he had passed mine.

The room felt soft.

My parents were united and in love, wishing me love. Parker was glad for me. And Blaize was relieved; Megan had not steered him wrong.

Ever so gently he slid a wrist corsage over my fingers and eased the elastic strap so it didn't bite my skin. His hands held mine only for a moment, but it felt like the touch I had been waiting for all my life: concern and affection and interest and full of gifts to come.

And in the drive, waiting, was a long sleek black limousine.

My eyes met Mother's.

Her face was lit in sparkles, and she tilted her chin ever so slightly and pursed her lips in a tiny kiss to me. She was as thrilled as I was.

A dance.

A limousine.

A nosegay of flowers on my wrist and a handsome boy in a dark romantic jacket.

"Good night," I said to my family. Even my voice felt softer, my hand already in Blaize's. He was no stranger. His clasp was warm and strong as if he, too, had been waiting for this hand, this moment.

I smiled at Blaize and he smiled back and for an instant we paused in the door, already caught in romance.

I heard a sigh.

Parker. A sigh for love and its joys.

But tonight it was my turn.

CHAPTER

The limousine brought me home at quarter to midnight. It was the driver and not Blaize who walked me to the front door.

It was earlier than my family had expected and when Dad opened the door—because of course he'd been waiting up—he knew there was something wrong. I meant to go straight to my room and keep my sorrows to myself and say nothing ever. But I couldn't bear it. I told Dad everything. "Everything" took a short sentence.

"He didn't like me, Daddy."

Parents can't tolerate that kind of sentence. "Of course he did, Kelly," said my father. "He was just shy."

"No, Daddy. He didn't like me. He didn't talk or try to

get to know me. I was just a stuffed doll he towed around so he wouldn't be alone. He propped me up in front of his friends and especially his old girlfriend, but I wasn't special enough. He needed somebody really dazzling and I'm not dazzling. I'm just an ordinary pretty girl. I disappointed him."

My father dropped into his recliner and yanked me down on top of him.

I sat in my father's lap and wept into his heavy woolen sweater. Megan's lovely long gown was caught between us, dragging behind me like torn rags. I pulled off the wrist corsage and let it fall. All that was left of the evening was a painful red mark where the corsage band had gripped me too tight.

I don't like the recliner. It's big and ugly. But when Dad tilted back, I felt as if I were still his little girl. All my life I'd wanted to grow up and stop playing games and have the real thing. But the real thing hurt.

The real thing is being ignored. Not measuring up. Not being talked to. Not being danced with. "Daddy, I thought it would be perfect. It was all there. Flowers and a limo and music and a handsome boy. Romance is terrible."

"Aw, Kell." Daddy shifted me around so I was sitting next to him, squished up against the fat leather arm. We stared at the oil painting of the sea and sand that my mother bought years ago on their honeymoon—the view from their hotel. "Don't hate romance," said my father. "I'm into romance. I think it's neat."

"Not for me it isn't."

"Don't write it off just because of one lousy boy and one lousy night."

"But, Daddy, it was my first date. And what if it's my only date?"

"First dates are hard," he agreed. "Takes practice to figure out what you're doing."

"Blaize has had lots of practice," I said miserably. "And he didn't want to do anything with me but have me there."

"But he was so nice when he picked you up!"

All night long, Blaize had been showing off. He showed off to my family, to the chauffeur, whose services he had engaged when he was still going with Jill. That was her name, Jill; she was just like Wendy, a Queen of Romance. He showed off to his friends, to his teachers, to the chaperones and most of all to Jill. But he didn't show off to me. I wasn't worth it.

"The flowers were just flowers and the music was just notes," I said. "I was another purchase, like the corsage. But less successful."

Daddy smoothed my hair, always silken, always soft. Hair I had wanted Blaize to touch. "If he's that dumb, who needs him?" said my father.

"I need him. I want a boyfriend."

"Your time will come."

"Daddy, I can't stand it when you say that. I don't want my time to arrive out there in the future when I'm old. I want it right now, in high school, during my junior year, right this minute. I want it like Megan has it and Wendy has it and the way you and Ellen used to have it."

Oh, was I sorry I had said that. Now I couldn't even wallow in my own disaster. I had to think of my parents' misery as well.

"Sweetie, I learned a lot in those eight years with Ellen," said my father after a long pause. "You know I'm addicted to buying stuff. I just love to give presents. If I'm working all day, and the day is hard and rotten and I had to be nice to people I despise or work on a project I think is pointless or finish one I think needs another six weeks—well, it's so nice to do one thing right. Buy a long-stemmed red rose, hand it to your mother and see her light up. And I found out from Ellen that you can run a long, long time on romance. It can fuel years of dating."

The last thing I wanted was a heart-to-heart talk about Ellen. I wanted to talk about me. Was that so selfish? Once in sixteen years? To have the focus on me?

"But it can't supply love," my father finished.

Had Daddy bought Ellen? The way Blaize bought me? Flowers and music and great cars? And had Ellen let it go on for eight years because she liked dating, she liked attention—but she didn't love him and never had?

Incredibly, it was Ellen I agreed with. I wanted to flirt and be liked and have presents and dance gracefully with the handsome boy. I hadn't asked Blaize to love me, just have fun being with me.

And he couldn't be bothered. I wasn't worth his time. I was worth nothing.

I began crying horribly.

"You matter to me," said Daddy.

Every father in the world, and every mother, has tried to end a talk with that line. You matter to *me*, dear. *I* love you. So what if there's not a boy on earth who does? Your old daddy loves you and that's what counts, huh?

"You just have to get through it, Kell," he said, hugging me fiercely. "You'll feel better eventually and manage to be happy and there will be somebody there for you. I guarantee it."

"But, Daddy, some girls never find anybody. I don't want to be like them. I don't want to be a loser."

"Of course not. Everybody hates being a loser."

"It's worse than that. Everybody hates the loser, too. They don't associate with her and then she's even more of a loser."

The kitchen clock chimed the hour. My father's breathing was regular. He was all but asleep. The tears had dried on my cheeks and their tracks were itchy. "I'm stiff, Dad. I'm wrinkling Megan's dress. I'm going to bed."

He tilted the recliner forward so fast it flung me onto my feet. "I didn't have any words of wisdom, did I?" said my father sadly. "I'm sorry. I wanted to help."

"The only thing that could help right now is my phone ringing and some terrific boy telling me he adores me and he can't go another twenty-four hours without seeing me."

My father was laughing. "I could pay somebody off."

"That's like Megan fixing me up. I want it just to come. Like a door opening. Fireworks exploding." I could see it so well.

The door—a glimpse into an unknown room at the unknown boy who would love me.

The fireworks—seeing this unknown boy, feeling explosions and fire and laughter and joy.

"You are so like your mother," said my father, exasperated and affectionate.

Me? Eternally anxious? Hiding from reality? Busying myself with nothing much? Only smiling when Dad smiled first? Me?

"Kelly," said my father softly, "it's okay to be needy. It's okay to need love. You don't have to be sorry you need it. You don't have to fight back."

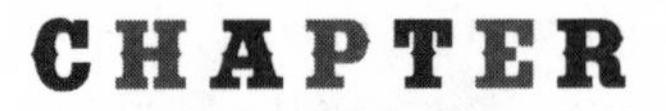

CHAPTER 10

"Kelly," said Megan, "you are blind. You need a guide dog for dating."

At least she didn't tell me I'm the dog, I thought.

I washed my hands. There's gray soap in the high school girls' rooms. I don't think a person can get clean with gray soap. It's a contradiction.

Megan sagged down the wall of the girls' room, sinking dramatically onto the tile floor. Her hair draped over some obscene graffiti.

"Don't do that," said Faith crossly. "They haven't mopped in here since Carter was president." Faith brushed her hair with such vigor that I cringed. If I were that rough, I'd be bald along with my other troubles. Faith never even notices the handfuls of hair she loses; she just fills the wastebaskets and moans about humidity and in the morning she has even more hair.

"Here I knock myself out to arrange the perfect evening for you, Kelly, with Blaize, who is also perfect, and you goof up."

"Oh, Megan, don't yell at me," I said, fighting tears. "Don't tell me I goofed up. Say we just weren't right for each other."

Megan drummed her heels against the tiles. She was wearing good shoes with tiny sharp metal points on the high heels. She lifted her knees ever so slightly and accomplished a sitting-down tap dance. I was filled with admiration for her coordination. "Kelly, you should not get so emotional. It was only a date. You should have laughed your way through a great evening. You're too intense. You cannot cannot cannot be intense about boys."

Then what's the point? I thought. Who needs romance if it's not intense?

Faith said mournfully, "I'm awfully emotional about Angie. Do you think that's why he doesn't respond? We had such fun at lunch!" A lunch that had to have been a month ago. "We flirted and giggled and joked and it was perfect. So why won't he ask me out?"

Megan heaved a huge sigh and began explaining in detail why Faith and I were failures at love. At first I listened, because I really wanted to know, but about ten syllables in, I saw that it was going to be too depressing, so I checked out. Megan punctuated her lecture with heel taps. She was ruining her shoes, getting scuff marks all over them. She didn't care. No boy would care either.

I stared at myself in the mirror. All bathrooms at Cummington High are gray like their soap. There was probably some huge sale on gray tiles and gray sinks when they were building the school. I was happy they had saved all that money, but tired of so much grim, dark, sad gray in my life.

I was even wearing gray. My oldest sweatshirt, the baggy one with words so faded that even I am not sure what they say. My oldest jeans, so pale they've become a reflection of my personality: pretend jeans covering a pretend girl.

If we stay in this bathroom much longer, I thought, I'm going to have a nervous breakdown. Maybe I'm already having a nervous breakdown.

"I'm having a nervous breakdown over Angie," said Faith, "and he doesn't even know it. I think of him every minute. Setting the table, doing math, watching TV, practicing the flute, and Angie is part of it. It's as if his invisible clone stuck to me with some terrible glue I can't melt."

I should add those to my board game, I thought. *Pointless Crush. Total Obsession. Unrequited Love.*

Megan took about fifteen paper towels to dry her hands. One high school junior cleans up and the trash overflows.

"It's my name," said Faith glumly. "I have this overwhelming need to be faithful. To have one guy in my life and love him forever."

Megan shuddered. "You're right. You're doomed. *They'll* never feel that way. If *you* do, it's over." She made it sound as if boys wanted paper dolls, one dimension.

"Let's go," said Faith. "Sociology next. We don't want to be late. Maybe Angie will ask me for lunch again today."

Perhaps it was Angie who was one-dimensional. His attitudes never changed; his charm never dwindled. But what was inside? Anything? Was Faith in love with nothing?

But in a really gray mood, you know that even love itself might be nothing.

The other two hurtled toward class. I trudged. I hadn't seen Will since the dance with Blaize. Now I knew that love was nothing, boys were paper dolls and I needed a guide dog. I certainly wouldn't have a crush on Will. I probably wouldn't even recognize Will.

That made me feel better. Strong. Independent. Calm. Poised.

In the doorway of the classroom stood Will.

The face that had seemed bony was now full of interesting angles and planes.

The eyebrows that usually expressed only conceit seemed inquisitive.

The face that was so snobbish had a stranded expression—one of somebody needing a friend.

Will looked at us.

Vibrant Megan. Faith radiating her crush on Angie. And me in my sloppiest sweatshirt with my grayest emotions.

"Hey, Kelly, how are you?" said Will, as if Megan and Faith were invisible.

"William, William, you're blocking the road," said

Megan, who cannot bear to be ignored and certainly not by a boy she herself just ignored.

"Fine, thanks, Will," I told him.

He nodded and went to his desk.

Only people who have suffered from really serious crushes—terminal crushes—know that a person can be wafted off for an entire class on "How are you?" and a nod.

I was wearing one nice thing: my gold chain with the eighth-note gold charm. I fingered it while I looked at Will, hoping for a glance or smile to confirm his interest. To prove he wasn't snubbing Megan, but was crazy about me. Will's interest, however, was in the lecture. He took notes. He did not look up.

I really care, I thought. Not so much about Will. Will and Blaize themselves hardly matter. I just want somebody to like me. I don't care anymore who does the liking. I am desperate.

What a terrible word in a girl's vocabulary.

". . . to be special," squeaked Ms. Simms. "You do library work, in your language arts classes and history. You translate paragraphs in foreign languages and attempt lab research in biology or chemistry. But for your sociology project, I want something special. Anything to do with the way one person interacts with another."

"The way boy interacts with girl?" piped up Angie.

"Of course. Male-female relationships are complex. Any data you can supply to help us understand will be greatly appreciated."

Angie beamed. "Then my project's finished. I've been working on it since my thirteenth birthday and I've already—"

"I think not, Angelo," said Ms. Simms. "Sexual expertise or the complete lack of it will not be considered."

Angie's all show! I thought. He fooled everyone but Ms. Simms. It's not that the girls don't measure up to Angie's standards; it's that Angie doesn't know what to do next and he won't risk mistakes. Complete lack of expertise defines Angie.

"Project ideas must be submitted within two weeks. If you are late, the grade will drop ten percent."

Lots of people take sociology as an easy A to prop their grade point average up. Now they'd have to exert themselves, which caused classwide groaning. Even Wendy whined. "But Ms. Simms, I do so much creative stuff already. I don't have time to think up something *else* that's special and wonderful."

This time Will looked my way and we rolled our eyes at each other. Did Wendy Newcombe have a high opinion of herself or what?

Jeep spoke up on Wendy's behalf, wanting Wendy to be exempt from the project, or be allowed to submit a soap script.

Parker would have done that too, I thought. He's still on Wendy's team, even though I don't think she has a team. She's captain, but for herself alone.

I should put that on my board: a square to show that

sometimes you love a person for what doesn't exist. You'd have to pay a big penalty for that. Of course, you didn't need a board game to pay penalties. All you had to do was fall in love.

Romance was such a soft and beautiful word. In it were such hard and cruel divisions.

And suddenly I was laughing, almost exulting. My romance game would be my sociology project. Not only a class activity, but one about male-female relationships and the complexity thereof. Ms. Simms would love it.

The bell rang, the class vanished and I struggled to my feet. Skinny as I am, I should come out of a school desk like a trout through water, but I must have the wrong proportions. Never once have I stood up gracefully in school.

"I am dying to know what you're thinking," said Will, standing next to me. "The expressions that have been crossing your face in the last five minutes have been priceless. The trouble is, I didn't figure out a single one."

I blushed. "Hard to explain," I mumbled. Oh, no, I thought. I sound as if I don't want to share my thoughts with him. Megan's right. I do need a guide dog for romance.

"Wendy's kind of a jerk, isn't she?" observed Will, going with me to the door.

"I love hearing you say that!" I exclaimed. "You're so removed and objective. If you say she's a jerk, then she is."

"Me? Removed?"

We reached the hall.

"I'm sure your expressions meant something interesting," said Will. "Would you tell me over a Coke? This afternoon?"

CHAPTER 11

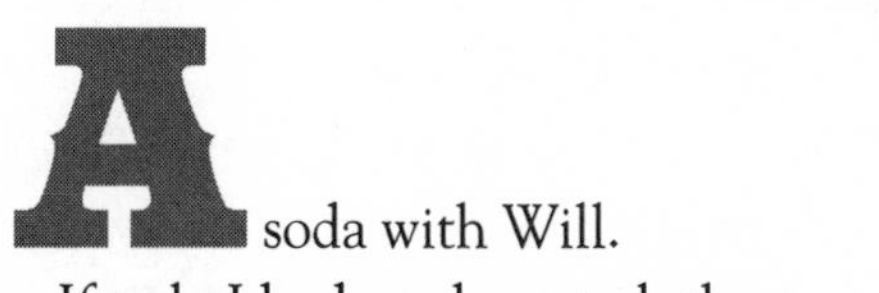

A soda with Will.

If only I had on decent clothes.

Of course I was in my worst sweatshirt and my oldest jeans for my first date. (I wasn't counting Blaize as a first date. He was a punishment.)

I dawdled, because I was afraid of Will. I had known him most of my life. Watched him in sports, where conceit serves him so well, and disliked him in class, where conceit is infuriating. What was there to be afraid of?

He was waiting for me in the front foyer. Why wasn't I running toward him, the way Wendy had run after Park and was now running toward Jeep? I wanted this so much: a boy asking for my company. It had come and I was dragging my feet.

A thousand times I'd listened to Megan talk about her boyfriends. Never had fear come into her conversation. Desire, worry, adoration, frustration, concern, but not fear.

"Hi," said Will, grinning.

There was no fear visible in Will. He is so tall that for him merely to stand there is to be on display. I felt as if the entire school watched me approach, saw my head tilt back to greet him. I'd always figured I'd love being on parade. But I was wishing we could be in private instead.

"Hi," I said, and blushed over the word *hi*, which I say to a hundred people every day.

"Let's go to Wendy's," he suggested.

I was shocked. Wendy's? Surely Will knew how mean she had been to my brother. Just a little while before, Will and I had agreed that Wendy was a jerk. Was the whole basketball team going out with Wendy? Was this going to be a double date with Jeep and Wendy? Was—

"Wendy's that serves hamburgers," said Will. "Did you think I meant Wendy Newcombe?"

"I guess she's on my mind."

"She doesn't deserve the space. Come on. My car's in the east lot because I was late this morning. We have a hike."

We didn't touch. We didn't walk close. In spite of being afraid, I was disappointed. As long as you're doing it, you should do it right. Tons of people were looking at us, or at least facing our way, and I wanted to give them something worth looking at.

Am I sitting on both sides of this fence or what? I

thought. How do I expect Will to have any idea what I'm thinking when *I* don't have any idea what I'm thinking?

My mind rushed down the paths of other minds, wondering what they were thinking, and constructing thoughts for them. My father's path, my mother's, Parker's, Wendy's, Faith's, Megan's—seeing with their eyes, deciding with their minds. I've always wondered if other people's minds do this—divide, splinter, race headlong in multiples. Or do other people always know who they are?

"You know, Kelly, I've come to a conclusion about you," said Will.

"What's that?"

"I figured you for solid as a rock but now I think you're kind of flaky. A lot of girls, I psych them out, I know who they are, and I'm bored. With you I have this feeling that you don't land. You only look as if you land. But really you're flying out there somewhere and you've never landed."

It was strange and glorious to find myself in Will's thoughts, to know that when his mind split, one path it took was through me. "I didn't know you thought about me at all."

"A person has to think about something during sociology," Will pointed out. "I've been working my way through all the girls in the class. Depends which way I'm facing. Like when I was facing Wendy, I spent a lot of time trying to figure out what game she's been playing with Jeep and Parker."

"Oh, me too. I'd give a lot to understand that."

Will opened the car door for me. I love little attentions.

I thought of the thousand little attentions Dad gave Mom and for the umpteenth time in a month I wondered about my parents. I prayed they weren't getting close to a—

The real word crept into my mind.

Divorce.

Horrible, evil word. I let it sit quietly and then I picked it up, like a stone, and flung it away as far as I could.

Will was still walking around the car. He got in on his side and put the key into the ignition, and the car began buzzing very loudly. "Put your seat belt on," he yelled.

I snapped it in place. "Our car has a sweet tinkling bell to remind you about the seat belts. Yours gets violent."

He started the engine. "Tell me why you want to understand Wendy. I'm not sure Wendy is worth understanding."

"Because of Parker. He's hurt."

"I'll bet. We could see it coming, but Park couldn't. You couldn't warn him or you'd be the enemy."

"Will you ever talk about it with him?" I asked.

"I hope not."

How I love girl talk. Sprawled on the bedspread, indulging in long intimate heartbreaking silly giggly friendly talks. Girls love telling all. We always tell all.

Or so I'd thought until I fell for Will. I hadn't told anybody about that. Not even Faith. For some reason, especially not Faith.

I was no longer afraid of Will. Talking released the anxiety. We arrived at Wendy's and got in line. Will touched me for the first time, hand on my waist. Not light, not a half tickle, but a firm palm that ushered me ahead of him. I asked for chili; he ordered four hamburgers.

"Four?" I said.

"A person gets hungry."

I gazed up at him and found him looking down at me speculatively, the way I might look at a dress I'm thinking of buying, but have not yet made the final decision on.

Nervousness came back like a blow. I was on the board game, getting and losing points.

Will's hand moved me forward again. The tray was handed over the counter and Will took it. One hand holding the tray aloft, the other at my waist, he walked us toward a table by the window on the far side.

No wonder my mother loved all the little things Daddy did. They made you feel special. And who could not want to feel special? It's so nice to be worth an effort.

Again my thoughts split away, abandoning my date. Opening doors, holding the tray, choosing the table. What could be wrong with it? What were Parker and I thinking of, knocking Dad for showing Mom affection like that? And whatever were Mom and Dad thinking of, letting it fade? Over Ellen! Who didn't matter to anybody!

Did Daddy still have Ellen's letter in his wallet? Was he still staring at her photograph? Was he sorry he was married to the mother of his children and not to this other woman?

"Now you have to tell me that," said Will. "I refuse to be left in the dark."

"That what?" I said, though I knew.

"That latest thought. Another intense one." He took the food off the tray and slid the tray onto a vacant table behind us. Handing me a napkin and a straw, he got to work on burger number one. Three bites, fifteen seconds, and he was washing it down with his soda, not even pausing for breath.

I was still lifting my spoon to approach the chili. "Wow," I said.

"I eat kind of fast."

"I guess so."

"But that doesn't let you off the hook. What were you thinking of that made you look so far off?"

I put the white plastic spoon into the chili, brought up a mouthful and lowered the spoon back into the bowl. I picked up a pack of crackers, although I don't like crackers and never spoil my chili with them. I played with the cellophane packaging.

"It's my parents. I thought they had the most beautiful marriage on earth. I loved thinking about the way they loved each other and how someday I would live like that. But now, for the smallest dumbest reasons, it's coming apart at the seams. Parker and I are standing there watching it split. It's happening so fast, as though it never had any strength, when I thought it was the strongest in town. Sometimes just one word in an ordinary conversation makes me remember what's going on with them and I get scared."

Will touched my hand. The cellophane rustled at the pressure. His hand dwarfed mine. The pressure of his fingers was comforting out of all proportion. "My folks are divorced and they remarried and they divorced again. You live through it. I won't say it's a picnic, but eventually everybody comes out on the other side without being destroyed."

"I don't want to think about it. I can't bear thinking about it."

"I don't imagine they want to think about it either."

"If my mother would just act like an adult, it could be solved in a weekend."

"What's she doing? Are you going to eat those crackers or not? The sound of the wrapper is getting to me. I really love crackers, you know, and if you're not going to eat those crackers, I'll eat the crackers."

I was hurt. I had been on the brink of sharing with Will what I hadn't even shared with my own brother: my ultimate fear. And Will interrupted to talk about crackers?

"Hey, you two," said Jeep, "why didn't you say you were coming over here? Hi, Kelly. Shove over, will you?"

He and Wendy, arms around each other, faces full of affection and laughter, were bouncing beside us.

I gave Will a look of heartfelt relief for babbling about crackers. What a gift. Otherwise my family problems would have been heard by the last girl on earth I wanted listening. Will nodded infinitesimally.

"Kelly, you change seats," ordered Wendy, "and sit next to Will so I can sit with Jeep."

Will gave me an I'm-on-your-team smile. I got up, feeling like a stick figure wearing rags, and circled the table while Will slid my chili, drink and crackers to my new place. Jeep and Wendy arranged themselves across from us. It was nice to be next to Will, but it meant I had to look at Jeep and Wendy.

How come Jeep didn't think that maybe Park's sister wouldn't be totally warm and friendly toward him? How come Wendy didn't guess that I hated her for throwing my brother over? How come Wendy didn't guess that I really really really hated her for using my intimacy quotient?

"I've decided to set next week's soap in an amusement park," Wendy told us, as if we were interested. "Jeep has recorded some great honky-tonk music for the merry-go-round and we've got wonderful screams for the roller coaster. I think I'm going to have the Ferris wheel break and Octavia fall off."

"Poor Octavia," I said. "She just recovered from her pregnancy. Now she's going to fall a hundred feet to a hideous splatty death next to the cotton candy? Don't do it, Wendy."

"I love it," said Wendy to Jeep and Jeep only. They squeezed a kiss between sentences. "Kelly takes this stuff seriously. She's really worried."

She's not a script*writer*, I thought. She's the script. She's a piece of paper. She just wants to be read by the world.

She doesn't care about her effect on living people, like Parker or like me.

"Do you realize that when you're having these heavy thoughts," said Will to me, "your mouth opens slightly and your eyes slip out of focus?"

"She doesn't have heavy thoughts," said Wendy. "She's got a weak jaw."

"Hey," I said indignantly.

"Watch it, Wendy," said Will, "or I'll have to throw chili at you and ruin your pretty sweater."

"It is a nice sweater, isn't it?" said Wendy contentedly.

Will and I laughed. He ate two more hamburgers, which kept him busy for the same number of minutes.

"I just want to go on record as saying I stand in awe of your burger-eating capacity," I said.

"And to think I was trying to show off by making baskets or As. All I had to do was snack." He ate the fourth burger. "Now I'm all sad."

"Because you have a stomachache from eating four hamburgers?" asked Wendy.

"Because they're gone. I love to eat. Wish I could make every meal last for hours." He eyed the crumbs from his rolls.

"This is not a high-tech solution," I said, "but you could try taking smaller bites."

Will laughed.

Wendy went back to her favorite topic (Wendy) and we listened. Jeep was not talking. He was sitting there, handsome as a soap opera star. Wendy was living out her own drama. Jeep was her male lead. And Parker had been what? Her twist in the plot?

Into my ear, Will murmured, "You have to control your face, Kell. It's impossible to tell what you're thinking, but you're definitely thinking something we'd all like to tune in on." His breath against my cheek and ear made me shiver. When I turned to smile, our lips were nearly touching. I counted the freckles on his cheek, measured his eyelashes, admired flecks in his hazel eyes.

"Come along, George Peters," said Wendy, which startled me because I never think of Jeep that way. "Things to do, people to see," she told us, taking Jeep's hand. They rushed away.

"Aren't people mysterious?" I said.

"There's nothing mysterious about those two. Wendy wants to run the world and Jeep's willing to be run."

Still and all, they were surely the most romantic-looking. A lot of kids were glad when Wendy went back to Jeep. It looked better, they said. Parker just wasn't her type.

Will was talking basketball. "We're in a battle between our two coaches. The head coach says it's enough to do your best; you don't have to win. The assistant coach says winning is the only thing that counts. Ever." He twirled my chili bowl. "You going to eat this?"

"No. Have it."

He ate my chili between sentences. "When we're at practice, I agree with the head coach. You do your best and it's enough." He crushed the crackers into the chili. "But when we're in a game, all I care about is winning. I love to win." His voice was as intense as Wendy's in a soap. "Winning is everything."

Winning.

The purpose behind every game, every crossword puzzle, contest, footrace or argument. "What is winning?" I said.

"Being first."

I wondered what it would be like to be first with Will.

"I'd like us to win the state basketball championship and have my jersey retired in the glass trophy case in the front foyer," said Will. He smiled at his daydream. "What do you want to win?"

"Happily Ever After." I was surprised and sorry I'd said it out loud.

He didn't laugh. He didn't get up to leave. His smile was sympathetic. "I've seen a lot of divorce. I guess I don't have much faith in happily ever after. A girl who wants that wants it all."

"But you see, I had it all. Or, at least, I thought my parents did."

"Maybe they do. Maybe this is a temporary lapse."

Will drove me home, enjoying the traffic as much as he enjoyed me.

And what was this afternoon, Will? I thought. Something real?

Or a temporary lapse?

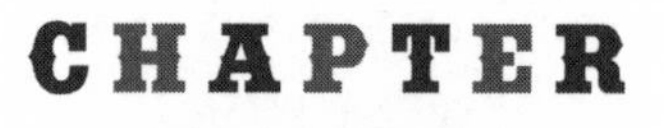

CHAPTER 12

You could look at me and see.

I couldn't see. I wore my favorite outfit but when I glanced in the mirror to check it, I didn't spot the difference.

In the first class of the school day, Faith said, "You look sparkly, Kelly."

"I do?" It's Will, I thought. I'm in love. "Maybe it's my shirt. This is my best color, you know."

Megan looked hard at me. "I suppose. But Faith's right, Kell. You seem bouncier than usual."

"I had a good night's sleep."

What a lie. I'd hardly slept at all. I lay there thinking alternately of Will and of me, layering us like lasagna: first the pasta, then the sauce. First Kelly, then Will, then Kelly, then Will, until we were one.

Forget the squares on my board, Will. Forget the skiing in Colorado and the cruise to the Bahamas and the hot-air balloon ride. Just telephone me. That's all I ask.

Around three in the morning I got out my romance game.

By now I had worked out a name system so you didn't draw a boy or a girl card but got a blank card. You had to fill in a name, and as you played, you landed on squares that built the character of your date by chance, and then you went out with him, thus collecting Traits and Dates.

I named my date Will.

Immediately chance turned him into a slob who had bad breath, drove a rusted-out station wagon and worked at a landfill for a living.

"Well, that's no fun," I said to myself.

This time I gave myself four dates to take around the board and named them all Will. Will One, Will Two, Will Three, Will Four.

And this time it worked the way a game should. It was dumb, it was funny, it had a nice pace, it made me laugh.

Will One never took me on a date. I'm sure he would have if he could have, but Will One never landed on a date square. My rule was that you couldn't go to Happily Ever After with somebody you'd never dated, so good-bye, Will One.

Will Two was rich, which was nice, but bald, which was

not. Will Two, in spite of being addicted to TV reruns, bought me a ski lodge and flowers.

Now, poor Will Three never developed any character at all. He dated me five times, so I could go to Happily Ever After with him, but who wants a future with a personality-free man?

Will Four.

Now, there was a man a girl could love. He was thoughtful, had high-voltage sex appeal, was a rock star with long blond hair and never complained. His only vice was that he slept with four dogs. Oh well, I told myself, it's probably a big bed. I can get used to the dogs.

I knew Will Four was the man for me when *Your date composes a love song just for you* appeared in his cards. I played slowly, hoping Will One would take me on at least one date and Will Two would land on a *Lose all vices—now your date is perfect!* Square.

At four in the morning, I landed on a Broken Heart.

♥

JUST LIKE LIFE!
WITH NO EXPLANATION WHATSOEVER
YOUR DATE DUMPS YOU FOR GOOD.
CRY ALL NIGHT.

♥

A jagged lightning streak ripped through the red heart drawn on the board, leaving one half bleeding on the ground.

Land on that square and whatever date number you roll next is off your list forever.

If I rolled Will One, it wouldn't matter, because he never took me out anyhow.

If I rolled Will Two, I could shrug.

Will Three had yet to develop personality, so presumably I wouldn't notice when he was gone.

But Will Four! What if I rolled a four? That would mean I'd have to keep playing the game with the other, lesser Wills and end up at Happily Ever After with one of them—or with nobody.

For some time I jiggled the die in my palm.

I would have said I'm not the slightest fraction superstitious. Certainly not while playing a board game that I myself invented.

But I never rolled that die. At four-fifteen in the morning I set the game back under the bed, dropped the die on the floor, turned out my light and never knew which Will would have been out of my life if I'd rolled one more turn.

But I did obey the square. I cried myself to sleep.

I don't even know why. Tears came. Not soft salty streaks on my cheeks, but terrible bitter sobs, as if something dreadful had happened and I just hadn't been told yet.

But all things are better in the morning.

I woke up happy, even with only two and a half hours of sleep. I dressed eagerly, glad to be able to atone for my baggy sweatshirt of the day before. Carefully I chose a plum-colored shirt loosely tucked into new vivid blue jeans. My hair looks like gold against that plum color. I could hardly wait to get to school. School would not be a board game. It was the real thing with a real Will, who really enjoyed me. Who really sat by me in sociology and had a real personality and really drove me to Wendy's and really was careful when people like Wendy were within listening distance.

I planned how to enter the room. After Will, not before. I'd be with Faith, although she wouldn't know she was an escort. I'd be very casual. Then I'd smile. Our eyes would meet. We'd have a secret interest in each other.

He'd pass me a note when Ms. Simms was hidden behind her papers. I'd send him one. He'd say, "That shirt is a great color on you." He'd text-message me on the phones we're not allowed to touch in class: "I have 15 minutes after school and before practice. Meet me. Student lounge."

I bounded down to breakfast and to a mother and father who were not speaking to each other. Whatever fight they'd had was over. They were in a state of truce, or else putting up a front for me.

My mother said, "Croissant, Kelly?"

My father said, "Orange juice, Kelly?"

My mother said, "Your father will drive you to school, Kelly."

My father said, "I don't believe I offered to do that, Violet."

Had this been going on for ages and I'd just never noticed? They sounded and looked as if they'd had plenty of practice behaving like this. "I can take the school bus," I said. Parker must have gotten an early ride with friends. There was no sign of him.

"You're late. He'll drive you," said my mother. Her jaw was set so tightly it hurt my mouth to see her teeth.

"No, it's okay. Really. The bus is fine."

"Whose side are you on?" demanded my mother.

We weren't even having an argument. I didn't even care how I got to school.

"She's not on a side, Violet," said my father. "There are no sides. Can you please grow up?"

"I believe," said my mother icily, "that that is what you need to do."

Thick angry silence again.

"What are we talking about?" I said. I wanted to think about Will and love and dates and flirting.

"I have no idea," said my father. "Get in the car. I'm taking you to school."

"I have meetings after work and into the evening," said my mother. "I won't be home for dinner."

"Neither will I," said Dad.

They both shrugged. They've been married so long their shrugs are identical, but they didn't notice.

In the car I said, "What's happening, Daddy?"

"Let's see. I'm going to buy a newspaper, go to work, and this evening, I'm going duckpin bowling with Charlie and Frank. Be home maybe ten o'clock."

"I mean with Mother."

He was furious. Not annoyed. Furious. "Kelly, stay out of it."

"Okay, okay. I was just asking. It's my family too."

"Some family," said my father as we pulled in front of the school.

It *was* some family. I had a lovely family. I adored my family. I wanted my family to last. Intact. In love.

I shivered all over. Dad saw nothing and drove away too fast.

The first three periods of school were torture.

A hundred times I silently practiced, "Hello, Will," trying to get exactly the right tone.

I dawdled behind Faith, getting to sociology almost last, sliding into my seat just as Ms. Simms was lifting her arm and placing her hand under her elbow. This is perfect, I thought. I get to send Will a quick grin while the rest of the class is getting out paper and pencil and nobody will notice and it will still be private and special and something to cherish.

What a game I was playing.

I waited for Will to turn in his seat so I could get past the silliness of the game and into the real thing. But Will did not turn and he did not look.

Not once.

All through class I kept turning toward Will, casually and slowly so the class would not notice, although I thought Will would. Faith was turning toward Angie in the same way at the same time.

We're like flowers, Faith and I, I thought. Turning toward the sun. Please shine on me.

But Angie was turned inward and Will was turned away.

Will gave me not one word, not one lift of his chin, not one half smile to indicate that we had ever associated or shared any thoughts or time.

Finally I stopped trying to catch his eye.

Idiot, I told myself. You spent a few minutes with a guy who's more interested in hamburgers and somebody else's chili. It was not a romance. It was nothing.

CHAPTER 13

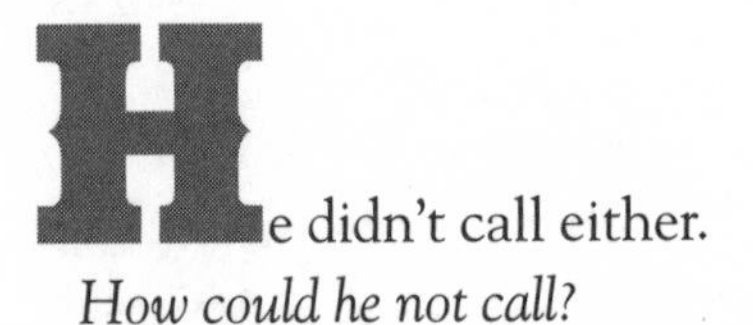

He didn't call either.

How could he not call?

We had shared so much and enjoyed the sharing so much. He had to call! He couldn't get along any better with any *other* girl. Megan hadn't ever gone out with him to start with. I didn't know if he had done much dating. But surely after such a nice time at Wendy's he'd have to call.

No.

The phone didn't ring.

Oh—it rang. Faith called with her usual monologue about Angie. I didn't say a word about Will. I still couldn't share him even with my best friend. Faith wanted the world to tune in to her needs. I

myself wanted no attention, no sympathy, no understanding.

I wanted Will.

The week passed.

School was hard.

Will would greet me in sociology and in history. "Hey, Kelly. How are you?" which was more attention than anybody else got from the guy, but still.

I'd answer, "Fine, thanks, Will." Which was a lie.

When he had a basketball game that evening, I'd say, "Good luck tonight." He'd nod and smile to himself, thinking of the game, not me.

In my heart I went back over every sentence we'd exchanged to see where I had gone wrong. If I studied my textbooks that intensely, I'd be graduating first in my class.

I went to two games. One was against Prospect Hill. Blaize was sitting on the away team's bleachers. In the last quarter, Will got sweaty and angry, leaping high for rebounds, sneakers squeaking, chest heaving. Nothing existed for Will but winning. And nothing existed for me but Will.

No cheers, no food, no gossip, no other people.

I knew now what Faith meant about her crushes. A clone of Will was clinging to me. An undercurrent to every thought and motion. It was like having company that never left. You loved them and hated them for giving you no peace.

Ms. Simms okayed the board game for my project. If I really thought I had something, she said, she would show me how to apply for a copyright. I said I didn't really think I had something.

I finished the board game on a non–basketball game night.

The board was remarkably pretty. I'd put a lot of effort into decorating and coloring it. Cut and traced a lot of folded paper hearts to get exactly the right sizes for the turns and curves of the game. Bought a lot of rubber stamps and experimented over and over with just the right bouquets and themes. The game was easy and fun to play. But then, I knew it by heart.

Good phrase. I didn't know the game by eyes, by mind or by fingertips. I knew it by heart.

It was the way I knew Will.

Not by intelligence or experience.

By heart.

Each day was the same. Either I was at school or I was at home. Either place, I was in the grip of this terrible crush on Will and he was in the grip of basketball.

One day I came home to an empty house and found on the hall table a vase of baby's breath, yellow daisies and white daisies. My father had tried flowers again. This made me feel slightly better. I wished I had been there when

Daddy gave them to Mother. How had she reacted? Had she kissed him? Exclaimed over the flowers? Hugged him and beamed with pleasure?

Or shrugged and said, "Stick 'em in water. I'm too busy."

I plucked one white daisy and began playing the oldest romance game in the world.

He loves me.

He loves me not.

He loves me.

He loves me not.

For whom was I playing this game? Me and Will? Or Mom and Dad?

He loves me.

He loves me not.

The petals fell on my lap like discarded chances.

He loves me.

He loves me not.

Half plucked, the daisy's yellow center became raw on one side and the stem seemed more fragile. I pulled off two more petals, counting to myself. If I looked at the remaining white petals, my eyes would do an automatic count and I would know the answer. *He loves me. . . . He loves me not.* I averted my eyes.

"Kelly!" called my mother. "I'm home!"

"Hi, Mom."

She walked in, saw the flowers I think for the first time and then saw the half-plucked daisy in my hand. "What are you on?"

"He loves me."

"Good place to stop. If you keep going, who knows where it might end?"

"There are only two endings," I pointed out.

"When in doubt, it's *He loves me not.*"

Oh, don't say it, Mother! Tell me that true love exists. Tell me you are proof of it. Tell me I will have it too.

"Who is the flower for?" asked Mom.

"Will Reed."

"As in basketball?"

"As in basketball."

Mother nodded, surprised but interested. Then she drew her own daisy out of the bouquet. A yellow one. My stomach clenched with fear. I had the sensation that if she plucked around and landed on *He loves me not,* she would leave. It would end: the marriage, the family—my life, her life, our lives.

She stared at her flower. "I never questioned it before," she said.

Daddy loving her? "But you always questioned it," I protested. "You always needed him to tell you he loved you."

"I know, but I didn't *worry*. I just liked to be told. Comforted."

"It's okay to need love," I said, repeating the only advice Daddy had to give his only daughter. It's okay to need love. You don't have to fight back.

So who was fighting back? Mother? Daddy? Ellen? Me?

Mother slid her yellow daisy back into the bouquet, lifting fronds of fern and baby's breath until it blended back into the crowd. We weren't going to find out whether he loves me or he loves me not.

I felt safe. We were still a family. That bouquet and all of us were still in the water together, still alive, full of color and hope.

"What?" I cried. "Never! Faith, I cannot telephone Will and Angie and ask them to come over to my house and play Romance."

We giggled insanely.

"You should have told me long ago that you had a crush on Will," said Faith. "I've always told *you* when *I* adore somebody. But when both of us are deep in fruitless hopeless crushes, we need a solution. This works. We coax Angie and Will to come to your house and play Romance."

I chewed my hair. Bit my fingernails. Twisted my socks. Picked at the seam in my denim bedspread. "I can't do it."

"Okay," said Faith. "Here's a possibility. We don't tell

them what the game is. We explain that you have designed a board game for the sociology class project and need to test it. You are throwing a game-testing party. Each person brings a good attitude and a sharp pencil."

I was getting sick of that bedspread. If I got up one more time and found seam lines imbedded in my skin, I'd set fire to it. "You know," I told Faith, "there's no reason I can't just go buy something new and replace this ugly thing. I'm thinking of a soft, puffy down comforter in pure white. I'll have about five throw pillows and they will be an array of—"

"Stop changing the subject. You're just chicken. Are we going to have this party or not? We need to invite twelve people so that we have three games going with four players at each board."

"I can picture two or three girls having a sleepover and playing this," I said, "but six guys and six girls in high school? Actually sitting down to The Game of Romance?"

"Yes. This is life, Kelly, and life depends on how you play it."

"You sound like pillow embroidery."

"We're going to play Romance and we're going to win. I get Angie; you get Will."

"Faith, what if nobody wants to come? What if they come and somehow I give everybody food poisoning? What if they laugh so hard at the whole idea of my game that they go into convulsions and can't play? What if my mother hangs around and acts weird?"

"Kelly!" shrieked Faith. "I myself with my calligraphy pens added that beautiful lace around the edges of your previously boring heart paths. I then paid for the color copies of your game. I glued the copies to heavy cardboard that I bought and cut out. I donated all my old Parcheesi game pieces and painted them in romantic nail polish colors for the playing pieces. I talked your very own mother into donating heart and violet gifts of your father's still in their packaging for door prizes. We are going to invite six boys and two of them will be Will and Angie and we are going to play Romance and that is that!"

So I picked up my phone and telephoned Angie first because I had no stake in the outcome of that particular call.

"Sweet," said Angie. "You are so clever, Kelly. Nobody else would be able to design a board game. What's the game about?"

"Secret."

"And I get to be at the unveiling? What time? You want me to bring something?"

"Just yourself." I left out the part about the good attitude, which Angie already had, and the sharp pencils, which I figured as hostess I probably should throw in myself.

All the calls went like that.

Megan was delighted, although irked that she wasn't in on the planning. "I'll bring paper plates and napkins," she said. "You might go for plain cheap white, because you think thrift is a virtue. I'll get beautiful romantic stuff."

"Don't tell anybody what the board game theme is, though. It's a secret."

"Oh, good," said Megan. "Because secrets are romantic too."

Kevin Carlson was astonished and pleased. "Me?" he said. "Sweet. What'll I bring?"

I had not expected people to offer to bring things.

"How about soda?" he said. "My family pretty much buys every kind of soda there is—no caffeine, high caffeine, no calories, low calories, classic original, whatever—I'll bring a cooler full."

Katy Ramseur was beside herself. "I'll bring dessert," she said. "I love to bake. I love to show off my baking."

Julie Tanner couldn't wait and was disappointed to find that somebody else had already offered to bring soda. She too would bring dessert.

Mario was confused but willing. He said he'd bring all the soft drinks. I said that was taken and he explained you could never have too much.

Honey under other circumstances would be low on my list, but we were limiting guests to the sociology class. Honey was actually polite and offered to supply chips and dips.

Donny McVeigh could not get over the idea that I was including him and was I serious? Did I really want him? Yes, Donny, I really want you. Sweet, he said.

"That's everybody but Will," I told Faith.

"Even with him, you're short one boy."

"Parker's coming," I said. "He knows about the game, he thinks it's cool, and he can be a host and take some of the pressure off in case I fly into a tailspin from public humiliation."

I couldn't bring myself to call Will.

"Kelly," said Faith. "Calling Will is the point."

"Leave the room," I said to her. "Go downstairs. Pray."

I called Will.

"Oh, hi, Kelly," said Will. "I was just thinking of you."

"You were?"

"Yeah. I'm getting started on my sociology project. Have you given much thought to yours? I've been so busy with basketball, I haven't had time to eat any four-hamburger snacks, let alone make phone calls, but how are you, anyway?"

"I'm pretty good," I said. My heart expanded, filling my body, taking up so much space, I felt like a helium balloon pulling on its tether. He would have made time for me if it weren't for games and coaches and practice! In truth, that was pretty lame, because two times a day, five days a week, we were in class together and a person could certainly say more than Hi, how are you? during those occasions, but I let it go. "Actually, Will, that's why I'm calling. I need special help on my project because it's a board game and I need to have four players at three different boards so that I can test it for flaws. Could you come over Saturday night? I checked to be sure—there's no game scheduled."

"I'm glad you're including me. Yes, I'll come. What's the game about?"

"Secret. What's your project about?"

"Not secret. I'm a Cummington native, the only one I know of. I'm going to find out what percent of the town was born here, and of the ones who moved here, I'm breaking it down into one year, five years, twenty years ago categories. I thought I'd also ask who plans to move on and when, so we can see how transient a town we are. Statistically correct phone poll. What do you think?"

"I think," I said, my mind racing forward at the speed of romantic light, "that we could do a second party for that. We'll ask everybody playing my game to show up another night and bring their cell phones and we'll have a poll party for you."

"Awesome!" said Will, laughing. "That would be so great. Because I don't really like the idea of calling strangers. Actually, I hate being on the phone. Maybe I can delegate phone powers and I'll just collate the answers."

"Then it's settled," I said.

"I'm on my way to the library," said Will, "because I need to look up any statistics they might have in annual reports and abstracts. Want to come?"

"Now?"

"Now."

"Yes, I want to come."

"I'm on my way."

Faith thought this was approximately a perfect conversation. I agreed.

Faith went home.

I was so buoyed up, I couldn't even stay in the house but went outside to sit on the curb and wait. The weather was raw and nasty but I had inner heat from excitement.

Parker suddenly appeared next to me. "Mom is hyperventilating," he said. "I can't stand it. I'm going to freeze out here with you instead." He sat down next to me.

"Do you think there's more to it than we know? Do you think Mom has some facts and some details that we don't know about and we don't want to know about either?" I said.

"Like a girlfriend? Like a long-term long-distance affair with this Ellen?"

"You wouldn't have said that so fast if you weren't wondering too."

"I think it's only Mom who's wondering," said Parker. "I don't believe Dad has done anything like that."

The cold came up into my body from the stone curbing.

Parker amended his statement. "I don't want to believe it, anyway."

"Did you tell Mom that's her same old ostrich-in-the-sand posture?"

"Sand is pretty nice, you know. Think Florida. A person gets a tan, does a little swimming, listens to the radio, checks out the girls. There's plenty to be said in favor of sand."

Will's car turned into Fox Meadow, past the silly development sign with its gold-leaf foxes playing in high green grass, past the first three houses, which were raised ranches, and into our section of houses, which were phony Colonials.

How tall Will was in that driver's seat. His head was pressed right up against the roof. We live just before the traffic turnaround, so Will passed me, turned around, came back and pulled up with the passenger door facing me. Parker opened the door for me.

"You coming as chaperone?" asked Will cheerfully.

"Nope. Just butler. Opening and closing the doors." Park went back in the house, and I knew that he was going to try to brace Mom and I loved him for it.

"I'm actually incredibly hungry," said Will. "I think it was the length of the drive over here. So before we go to the library, let's get hamburgers."

We went to the drive-in window and I had a small fries. I like to nibble, working my way up a single stick.

Will pulled into a parking space and ate pretty heavily until the edge was taken off his starvation. Then he turned sideways in the driver's seat, leaned back against his door and said, "So what's the board game?"

Right away I knew that front seats of large SUVs did not qualify as romantic. We were very far apart. We both still had our shoulder straps and seat belts on. Between us were enough cup holders for a basketball team who drank only supersize.

I leaned toward him for a little more intimacy. The strap held me when I'd gone halfway.

Will leaned toward me. His strap held him.

I arched beyond the grip of my shoulder strap.

He arched beyond the grip of his.

"It's good you're so tall," I said to him. "I think we may actually meet in the middle."

"It isn't really the middle," said Will. "I'm way over into your territory."

"One more inch," I said to him.

He covered the final inch. Our lips met. The kiss was salty and ketchupy and perfect. We kissed away the salt and kissed again and then Will straightened up, and when I started to straighten, the seat belt caught and hauled me back, like a chaperone displeased with the activity it saw.

"We'll get back to that," said Will. "It's better in installments. So you're not going to tell me about the board game. How's your family? Get that out of the way and we'll have our second installment."

"You're kind of pushy," I said.

"All that basketball. Working on my offense. Come on, spill it."

I spilled it. Will was a better listener than Faith, who gets so involved that it doubles my anxiety. Better than Megan, who accuses me of things such as needing a guide dog. "It's a flimsy marriage after all," I said finally. "When I thought it was all romance."

"I think it's very romantic. Your father accepts his wife's

insecurity as part of life and he's been nice about it year in and year out. That's true love. He's willing to sacrifice financially, and emotionally he's willing to spend lots of time. I suppose maybe she could use counseling, but they used romance instead, and it worked."

"Till now."

"I bet when they're at dinner with Ellen, your dad will go out of his way to be terrific with your mother, and keep his arm around her, and open doors for her, and tell great stories about how great she is."

"But I don't want a wimpy mother."

"At least you've got a strong father."

"And what if my mother's view is right? What if he's had an affair and she has reason to be afraid and the flowers are all some kind of cheap bribe?"

Will had some fries. "You're making that up. You don't have a bit of evidence. You're just trying to justify your mother's behavior. If I were you, I'd rather believe my mother was insecure and dumb than believe my father was sleeping around." Will fed me a fry and I ate it down to his fingers, and his fingers wandered over my face and held my cheek. "So what's happening at the party?" he said.

I was glad to drop the problem of my parents, but not glad when his hands dropped back to his food. "We'll play the game and see if it works and if it's fun," I said, "or if I need more stumbling blocks or more chances to accomplish things or more squares because it goes too fast, or if it's better with two players at a board instead of four. So people have to be critical, or I won't learn anything, but they can't be very critical or I'll cry."

Will laughed. "I'll stay in the noncritical camp. That looks safer. You know, Kelly, you're a mystery to me."

"A mystery? I'm an open book. I've told you things I haven't even told Faith."

"Really?" Will was immensely pleased. He savored that. "You've told me things your best girlfriend doesn't know? I thought girls shared everything. That's one of the things that make me so nervous when I face packs of girls."

I could not imagine Will nervous about anything. "Kelly Williams, woman of mystery," I said. "It has a nice ring. But maybe we should head for the library, because it sounded as if you had a lot for us to work on."

"I don't have any interest in working on anything at the library and I never did," said Will. "It was a ruse to get you in the car with me."

Boys.

They are all men of mystery.

CHAPTER

"Mother? How could you? After I swore you to secrecy, you went and told the whole town?"

"It wasn't the whole town. It was just Katy, Kevin, Donny and Julie. I ran into them at the mall."

"I can't stand it. They'll laugh at me. They'll tease me. They won't even come now! They'll be embarrassed to play a game of romance. I'll be embarrassed. I'll die."

Mom thought that was a bit dramatic. She made a face at me and drove slower. The more she talks, the slower she drives, so that if she's really involved in her story, you're crawling along, an accident waiting to happen.

"What time was this?"

"Maybe five o'clock."

"It's seven now. All Cummington knows I invented a romance game. By nine the entire state will know and by eleven o'clock the national television networks will be preparing a feature."

"But if you're going to market the game nationally, isn't that what you want?"

"I want to be in control of my own fate," I said.

"Good luck." Mom turned into a vast parking lot. Cummington has many malls, none of which has enough parking, except this one, which has ten times the parking it needs. There's always a sea of black pavement waiting to be parked on. But it was the end of January, and pockets of old snow and slick spots of ice reached out to ruin your footing.

The pharmacy at this mall carries everything from closet dividers to picnic baskets. I went to the candy section. I didn't really like Faith's game pieces. The nail polish had not stuck very well to the painted Parcheesi pieces and they looked—well—cheesy. I was going to buy a big bag of those tiny pastel valentine hearts that say LUV ME TRULY and BE MINE and I'd cover them in clear nail polish so they'd last for the evening and remind people not to eat them and they would be perfect game pieces and nobody could mix theirs up with anybody else's.

My mother went to look at greeting cards. I could see her way down the aisle, fingering card after card. Was she buying Dad a Valentine's Day card? An "I'm sorry" card? Should I buy Will a Valentine's Day card, and if so, should it be mushy or literary or slapstick? Did they have cards that said, "I hope you really do love me, because if you don't, I'm going to die"?

I hoped Mom was choosing a card that said, "I love you completely; let's kiss and make up and have everything the same as before."

I bought a very large bag of hearts. Either nobody would come to my party at all now that Mom had said what the game was about, in which case I could console myself for a long time popping candy hearts, or everybody in town would come, in which case I would need this many hearts.

Mother went to the checkout counter and I followed. "Let me see our card," I said.

She showed me willingly. A soft photograph, blurred like watercolor, of two people in a canoe, drifting beneath a weeping willow. It was very romantic. I couldn't wait to read the verse, but inside, it was blank. "You couldn't find a verse that fit?" I asked her.

"I think this time I have to write my own."

There were episodes in my life lately that nobody knew about. Mom, Dad, Faith, Megan—they hardly knew a thing about Will. Parker knew a little. What episodes in Mom's life did I not know about? As she and Dad drew closer and closer to Ellen Day, what was happening between them?

It was amazing how we could live under the same roof, share the same genes and meals and furnace, eat the same snacks, use the same sinks and glasses and stairs and yet be so separate. Glimpsing each other's pain or joy, but sideways, catching only shadows and reflections.

Mom and I returned to the car. Nobody was parked around us. Nobody was parked anywhere. It was a marvel the mall was still in business.

"Candy hearts?" said my mother. "Oh, perfect. You drive, Kelly. I want to pick out the best hearts to tuck in my card."

My real heart soared. We opened the bag carefully, so the hearts wouldn't spill, and my mother sorted through, eating some, throwing some back and cupping a few in her palm, where I couldn't read them.

"Are you choosing I'M YOURS and FOREVER YOURS?" I said.

She had chosen four of the same slogan, one each in pale pink, pale yellow, pale green and pale blue: I LUV U.

I thought of all the questions I would like to ask.

All the answers I would like to have.

All the interrogating I would like to do.

All the advice I would like to pass on.

But instead I turned left toward Fox Meadow, and when I came to a red light and stopped the car, Mom held up the candy bag for me to choose. I chose a heart that said I'M 4 U and I gave it to her and she said, "That goes right in my bloodstream," and she ate it and we laughed.

When we got home, my mother said, "Relax, Kell. We had a rough spot, neither of us handled it very well and now we're past it. Since you're spending every waking moment working on romance right now, I'll tell you that romance is something you can see, like a note tucked under your pillow. It's something you can smell, like a bottle of fragrance or a bouquet of lilacs. It's something you can wear or taste or show off. But love—it doesn't package well. You can't tie it up with ribbons and bows. You couldn't make a board game of love. Love won't sit in neat little squares and pause obediently for other people to take a turn."

She slid her hearts into her greeting card and slid her card into its envelope, but she didn't seal it. Her words weren't written yet and her signature wasn't there yet.

"But only love," she said finally, "is worth playing for. Worth working for. Fighting for. And even yielding for."

We went into the house silently. I felt better than I had in weeks. Maybe part of love is silence, I thought.

But silence made me think of my cell phone, which had not been ringing, and if Mother had really told the entire town, it should have been ringing steadily, so I pulled it out of my purse and looked to see if anybody had called, because sometimes love is a telephone that rings for you.

CHAPTER 16

The first guest drove up while Parker and I were still setting out the games on the floor because we didn't have four large tables in one room.

"This is high risk, Kelly," said my brother. "You're setting yourself up to be taunted by all these kids. You're baring too much of your soul."

Of course I had not slept all night, thinking the exact same thing, but I bluffed. "Don't you want me to make a success of this and have it become a nationwide fad and make us zillionaires?"

"Sure, but I want you to do it anonymously."

"I don't think romance can be an anonymous activity."

The doorbell rang. I got uncertainly to my feet and Parker called, "Mom, get the door, will you?" To me, he

said, “Kelly, you have a HUG ME heart stuck to your cheek. Is that intentional?”

I touched my cheek, and the candy fell into my palm. I didn't know whether it was intentional. There was certainly one person I hoped to hug in the course of the evening.

“Why, Katy!” cried my mother. “How lovely to see you! Come in!”

“I adore the color you're wearing, Mrs. Williams,” said Katy. “Now, where have you been all winter? You haven't come to a single basketball game. Don't you have any school spirit this year?”

My mother chose not to enter a discussion of where she had been and in what spirits. “What a beautiful cake!” she exclaimed.

“After you told me this would be a romance game, Mrs. Williams, I had to rethink my dessert plan. I've been icing this cake all day. I went for hearts and flowers.”

Parker and I caught up to the action. Katy's cake was a work of art. It was a glorious sheet cake, with icing an inch thick, ruffled with colors, cornered in hearts, beribboned and clumped with icing roses.

“Wow,” said Parker reverently, already pushing a finger into the icing for a taste. Katy just grinned.

“Kevin!” cried my mother, loudly, so that Parker and I would recognize a cue when we heard one and remember that we were hosting this party, and not Mom. “This is going to be such fun!” said Mom. “How are you, Kevin?”

"Hi, Kevin," said Parker. "Look what Katy made for our dessert."

Kevin was suitably impressed. "It isn't a white or yellow cake underneath, though, is it?" he said anxiously. "Romance cakes have to be chocolate, don't they?"

"Absolutely," said Katy. "In fact, I think true romance calls for eating dessert prior to eating the meal, so if you'd like to start, Kevin, especially since Parker has already started, that would be very romantic of you."

Kevin felt he could handle that degree of romance. He and Katy headed for the kitchen, a cake cutter and plates, although Kevin felt able to handle his cake without a plate or fork or even a napkin. Katy explained that just putting his face down in the cake and snarfing it up was not romantic.

Megan came racing across the yard and slammed into the house the way she always does, as if she's some four-wheel-drive vehicle attacking a cliff. Angie came a minute later, Donny, Julie, Faith and Will hot on his heels. Parker and I were so busy saying hi that Mom remained on door duty. "Mario!" she cried. "Honey! I guess everybody wants to be on time for romance."

There was an edge of hysteria to our laughter. We were embarrassed. But my mother handled romance with the ease of one who has spent two decades swinging it around.

Katy and Donny and Kevin began guessing what a romance game involved. Kissing each other? Adding clothing to become brides and grooms? Stripping off clothing to become brides and grooms at some point after the ceremony?

"I bet we're going to do an inventory of our hearts," said Katy.

I liked that a lot. An inventory of the heart. As if your heart were an attic, cluttered with trivial crushes and affections, but somewhere in there, one large trunk was packed with true love.

Will was grinning at me. He stood head and shoulders above most of the crowd, although head only above Mario and Angie, and his eyes were fixed on me. The angles and lean lines of his face, like the face of a very young Abraham Lincoln, smoothed away and became infectiously happy. He edged toward me. I edged toward him.

Although it was midwinter and winter colors are dark, all the girls had chosen to wear pastel. I love it when nobody plans in advance but everybody matches. It's like cars on the turnpike driving in clumps or everybody naming their babies the same thing. My year it was Jessica and Michael. For my party, group telepathy had put the girls in mint green, pale yellow and dusty pink. The boys, however, wore jeans and heavy sweaters in navy or gray, as if they had known they would need solidarity to play romance with girls.

When we were ready to sit down at the game—Katy's cake half eaten and the chips and dips totally ignored—people were nervous.

"How's it work?" said Angie. His jaw clicked to the side. Perhaps he was afraid of exposing a vein of ignorance.

"We divide into three groups of four each," I said. "Two girls and two boys per game. Nobody sits with a girlfriend or boyfriend because it will inhibit you."

They circled the game boards solemnly, counting out, following rules, looking like candidates for an ulcer screening. Honey said, "But there's nothing on the game board."

"It's upside down. Don't touch it yet. This is an unveiling and we're not ready to unveil. First, everybody sit."

"Wait!" cried my mother. "Don't start yet. Here comes another couple."

I frowned. Everybody was here. Faith and Parker and I moved toward the front window to see who it could be.

It was Wendy and Jeep.

Crashing my party.

The nerve! To come to the home of the boy she had just thrown over to play out a script of her soap opera. To a party she undoubtedly wanted solely as material for that soap opera.

Wendy bounced up our sidewalk, flirty and unselfconscious, while Jeep, handsome and perfect and outshining Parker, admired her progress.

I went to the door to shove them down into the pricker bushes but Parker beat me. "Come on in," he said cheerfully. "How are you, Jeep? Wendy? You almost missed the start of things."

"Give me a break," said Faith from the game room. "They're *trying* to start things."

Parker shot Faith a grin as he ushered Wendy and Jeep

into our house. The grin caught at me. It was not brotherly. It was a boy exchanging a look with a girl.

Wendy waltzed into the room where she had no business being and sat on the very sofa where she had passed many an hour with Parker.

Katy, who has never had any use for Wendy, said, "There is not room for two more players, so you might as well stay on that couch and be silent observers."

I decided it was time to be better friends with Katy. She was an ideal person. Baked outstanding cakes, considered chocolate romantic and put Wendy down.

But Parker said, "Having four people to a board is arbitrary and we don't know yet how many can easily play the game at one time, so we can probably work Wendy and Jeep in."

Four was not actually arbitrary. The game board had four sides, so it was going to work best with four people. But I let it go.

"I'll sit out the first game and go around getting people their drinks," said Parker. "Wendy, you sit over here by Julie. Jeep, you're next to Angie. We'll just have five at your board."

"We want to sit together," said Wendy, lip out in a pout.

"Against the rules," called Will. "Boyfriends and girlfriends can't sit at the same board."

Wendy plopped down where Parker had told her to. It was the only really bad position in the room. There was no place to rest her back and no floor pillow because Julie had taken two and didn't look as if she was giving one up to Wendy, and the boys at that board—Mario and Kevin—were personality-free (Mario) and also not fond of Wendy (Kevin).

Angie scrunched over to let Jeep sit down, so Faith was now squashed against Angie, which had been her master plan. "Angie," Faith said flirtatiously, "you can't sit with a girlfriend."

He laughed at the joke. "We're fine, then, because I've never had one. Never plan to. I'm not made for the game of romance."

The boys dropped to the floor with thuds that shook the lamps on the end tables. Katy and Julie pretended to be shaken by earthquakes, giving little shivery aftershocks and giggling. Faith, for whom it *was* an earthquake, had tears in her eyes.

"Faith," said Parker, "how about you sit out the game with me, instead of Kelly, and pass out pencils and paper and help me with the drinks. Please?"

"Pencils?" said Donny, worriedly. "Is this an exam? Do we get graded on how romantic we are? I'm leaving. I'd rather have my teeth drilled."

It was good cover for Faith's exit to the kitchen and a tissue.

"No," said Parker, surpassing any expectation I might ever have had of brotherly love, "this is a great game. You're going to have fun. Trust me."

When Faith came back, he gave her a hug. In a lifetime of living near each other in Fox Meadow, Park had given Faith many a thump, a scolding and a shove. But this was a hug.

What if a romance flowered during a romance game? Wouldn't that be wonderful? Wouldn't it be the seal of perfection on my game? There might even be two romances, because Katy and Kevin were looking at each other the same way that Faith and Parker were. Breathless and eager and hopeful.

I wanted to stand there and watch things unfold, but people were waiting. Expecting fun. My stomach clenched.

"Okay," I said. "Everybody get a pencil and everybody get a scorecard. You have six name slots on your scorecard. You have to make up names to fill in. Every girl fills in six boy names and every boy fills in six girl names. These are your potential dates. You cannot choose the name of anybody in this room. I'm going to make up different name-choosing rules for each set of players. Board One players may use any name. So a girl might choose Mitch, Jonathan, Jason, Dave, Lance and Rob, while a guy might choose Michelle, Jessica, Kathleen, Andrea, Molly and Ethel."

"I don't want a romance with a girl named Ethel," said Will.

"Who do you want a romance with?" said Wendy. "Somebody named Michelle or Jessica?"

Our school is packed with girls named Michelle or Jessica.

"No," said Will. "Somebody named Kelly."

For an instant nobody reacted.

Then it hit. Katy gurgled with laughter, Parker raised his eyebrows, Angie snorted, Donny looked delighted (but then, Donny always looks delighted), and Kevin said, "Sweet."

I focused on my list of instructions and tried to breathe.

"This romance game works fast, Kelly," said Wendy. "You have drugs in the soda maybe? Hypnotic suggestion in the pencils?"

"Only *you* have to resort to that kind of thing," said Katy. "The rest of us use personality and character."

Everybody howled. But Wendy's self-image is so great that she could laugh it off. Jeep didn't defend her, perhaps because he agreed or perhaps because he thought it was funny.

But Faith said, "There's a rule. Anybody who digs a knife into anybody during a romance game will never ever get to Happily Ever After."

"Oh, no!" said Katy. "I withdraw my knife."

"Happily Ever After," said Will. "I might have guessed that's where we're going." He was grinning at me and I thought, Who needs a game? I just want to think of Will and be with Will and plan for Will and dream of Will and then actually really truly *have* Will.

Instead I moved to the next set of players. "You guys will choose the names for the person on your left. So Julie chooses for Kevin, and so forth."

"Okay, Kevin," said Julie instantly. "I'm giving you two sexy names—Jody and Laurie. Two basic names—Catherine and Lee. And two loser names—Olga and Hortense."

Kevin said, "Then I'm giving you Percival and Dudley."

"You don't get to choose for me," said Julie. "The person on your left is Wendy."

"Oh," said Kevin happily. "Wendy, you get Percival and Dudley."

"Okay," said Wendy, surprising me by jotting down *Percival* and *Dudley*. "Those are my two loser names. What are my two sexy names?"

This group was obviously going to do fine. I moved on to game three. "You guys have to choose names alphabetically, so you might choose Anne, Bonnie, Claire, Deborah, Emma and Francine. Or Aaron, Burt, Chad and so forth."

"Can I start my alphabet where the last person left off?" asked Honey. "So I start with G?"

"Sure."

For a while there was no sound except the scrawl of pencils and the occasional whisper, "I need another name. Think of another name for me."

Parker carried a tray of sodas around while Faith stooped over each person with a bowl of chips and dip. Nobody wanted food. They were too involved with future boyfriends and girlfriends.

When all the players had straightened up and had a sip of their drinks, I said, "Okay. Turn your boards over."

There before them lay my precious game. Interlocked hearts, bouquets of flowers and the elusive Happily Ever After.

"Oh, Kelly, it's beautiful!" cried Katy. "It's a match for my cake."

"It's fabulous," said Wendy, unable to believe that I could be capable of anything fabulous.

"Oooooh, this is going to be so much fun," said Julie.

The boys remained silent.

"Now, the game is played with one die. Each turn, you'll throw it two times," I said. "The first throw is the number of spaces your game piece moves. Let's say you throw a three and you land on a heart card. You take a heart card from the pack and it will list six things. You throw your die a second time and the number that comes up is the number of your date. So if you wrote Jody under number one and you throw a one, then number one on the card describes Jody. Number one might drive a Humvee or be rated medium sexy. But number one might have eight hundred zits or never brush his teeth. You have to list that under your date and build your date's personality as you go."

"Can we discard dates that never brush their teeth?" said Wendy.

"You cannot dump anyone," I said. "You can only *be* dumped." Actually, this wasn't true, as some of the Broken Heart cards called for disposing of hitherto perfectly delightful people. But I couldn't resist.

"Stop talking," said Donny crossly. "I'm ready to play."

"Wait, wait. I have more directions. There are also yellow rose spaces. Each of these is a date, not a trait. The date cards describe what you do on this date. The object of the game is to reach Happily Ever After. You can't go to Happily Ever After with a person you have not dated, so if you never have a date with one of your names, you can't end with that date no matter how terrific he turned out to be."

They were all studying the board, calculating what might happen to this name or that one, reaching for the cards to shuffle through the possibilities and see what was in store for them.

"What are the hearts with the slashes?"

"Broken Hearts. That's when things go bad. You roll your die and whatever number comes up, it applies to that number date."

"Oh, no," said Katy. "This is too real."

"Stop talking," said Donny again. "Let's play. I'll go first at my table."

So they played.

I hoped for a good verdict on my game. I knew my premise was good. I just didn't know if my game itself was good. Would they get sick of writing things out? Would it go too slowly or would they fly on to the final square without managing to build characters for their dates?

But I already had one verdict that mattered.

Will was on my side.

And I already knew a bit about his character. And about Parker's, and Faith's, and now Katy's, and Kevin's, and Donny's.

I looked over at Will.

He had been looking at me all along.

CHAPTER

Did any hostess ever give a more successful party?

How many people can dish out love and romance along with cake and ice cream?

We finished one round of games and Parker and Faith joined the next round.

Katy had a splendid date named Zane, whose personality developed so well that Katy wanted his phone number, and we were cheering her on to Happily Ever After.

Faith had two nice young men with a relatively low number of vices, Adam and Brandon. Adam took her on outstanding dates while Brandon showered her with gifts and flowers. But she ended up in Happily Ever After with Clarence, about whom nothing was known except that he had a nice smile and large feet.

Wendy's dates were glorious. She was always off mountain climbing or partying with famous rock stars. But in the home stretch, she landed on Broken Hearts and was out of the game.

Parker drew a very nice and strikingly lovely girl named Celeste, but she had one awful characteristic: She put him down in public. But she was the only one of his dates who could go with him to Happily Ever After. "I am not going to Happily Ever After with a girl who puts me down in public," Parker kept yelling. Then, with his last throw of the die, he landed on a Lose All Vices square, so Celeste became perfect, and sighing with relief, Parker took Celeste on to Happily Ever After.

"I had a great time, Kelly," said Donny, when the game was over. "I wish I really knew Christie and Bitsy. I wouldn't have minded going around the board a second time with them and having a few more dates. Thanks for including me."

"Me too," said Katy, who was getting a ride home with Kevin instead of calling her parents. "A great game, Kelly. Parker is right. You have to get this thing produced by a real game board manufacturer."

I beamed at her. "Thanks for the cake."

Wendy surprised me the most. "It's good, Kelly. Sometimes you don't step forward when you ought to. Stop being a wallflower. Get out there and accomplish things. You're good. This game is more than good; it's wonderful. Go for it."

When she and Jeep were gone, Will said, "I don't like to side with Wendy, but she's right. Go for it."

Are you *it*? I thought. Are you what I should go for? Or is everybody referring to the board game?

"How did you fare, Will?" asked my mother. "Did you fall in love and arrive at Happily Ever After?"

Will's eyes never left mine. "I didn't progress quite that far."

Don't play games, Will, I thought. I want this to be real.

"It's not that late, Kelly," said Will. "I feel like a movie. There must be something at Cinema Six we could go see."

I didn't even have time to shriek with joy. My father, who had kept a low profile during the party, interrupted. "Nobody is going anywhere until this room is cleaned up. You may not leave this mess for us."

I hadn't noticed the mess, because to me the room was a thing of beauty, filled with laughter and friendship and fun. But how right he was. Pencil stubs and empty soda cans and broken taco chips were everywhere. There was a lot of work to do. My heart sank.

"Kelly and I will clean it up," said Will. "You guys go on into the kitchen and play another round of Romance."

"Good idea," said my father, herding Mom and Parker and Faith ahead of him. "I haven't played it yet."

"I'll pick your names for you," said Faith. "Yolanda. Eunice. Bunny."

My father laughed. "I'll pick my own names, thank you.

Number one will be Vi. Number two will be Violet. Number three will be Viola. Number—"

"That's against the rules," said Faith.

"Well," said my father, "in real-life romance, as opposed to board games, you get to make your own rules. And I play the game of romance with Violet."

When the door was closed, Will was frowning at it. "Your father didn't care enough about your board game to try it?"

"I didn't show it to him. He's been kind of negative toward romance lately, remember."

"Oh. I like him again, then. I was afraid he didn't want to bother with what his daughter did and then I wouldn't have any use for him. On the team, three of us have parents who never miss a game. It can be thirty miles away in the hills during a snowstorm and our parents get there. My parents come, and my stepparents and usually my ex-stepparents. They even sit together. My ex-stepmother is the one who always knows my stats. But some guys, their parents never come. Like Angie. I don't know his mother and father." Will reflected. "But I know they're no good."

I was staggered.

Poor Angie! A mother and father who cared so little, they couldn't be bothered to show up when he played varsity? No wonder he was jumpy with girls. He must not even know what love really is.

How lucky I am, I thought. I know what love is. And Will, whose parents and stepparents seem to come and go, he knows what love is. They've never stopped loving him.

I have to redesign the board, I thought. There's so much that I left out. All that I've learned from Will, my parents, Parker, Faith—even Wendy. But perhaps on a mere piece of cardboard there isn't room for even a fraction of what love is.

Will and I cleaned up.

I vacuumed.

He took out the garbage.

We surveyed the room.

We sat down on the sofa.

We looked at each other.

"Aaaaaah," said my brother. "Come into the living room to find a little privacy of our own and what do we find instead, Faith? People making out all over the place."

Will and I hadn't even touched yet.

"So how about the movies after all?" said Parker. "The four of us." He grinned at me. "You still get the backseat, Kelly."

"But the company in the backseat," Will assured me, "will be pretty good."

We headed for the front door, and I looked in on my parents as we left. They were playing the game. They were laughing. They were back at the Start Heart. I liked them in that square. It fit.

CHAPTER

Parker said, "I was on the phone with Wendy."

"Wendy!" I said. "I thought you were over her!"

"Relax. She and I are in charge of fund-raising for the class trip. Car washes, bake sales and dances are not going to bring in enough money. So Wendy had a fantastic idea." My brother put both his hands on my shoulders. Since Will was standing behind me with both *his* hands on my shoulders, I was trapped.

"I'm not a senior. What do I care whether your class takes a trip?" I said.

"Wendy wants us to act out the board game. Real people will pay for tickets and be real players. We'll chalk the board game out on the high school parking lot. We'll set up Romance booths. We'll sell roses and balloon

bouquets and raffle off dinners for two. Wendy thinks we can make a ton of money, because people will pay anything to get a little romance in their lives."

Who could resist?

Wendy organized it all.

Make a note of this: If you want publicity, choose a girl who loves the sound of her own voice. Wendy got free radio spots and local TV spots because sponsors loved the concept. We had four newspaper interviews and the usual posters tacked to every telephone pole for miles. And when the day came, practically the whole town showed up. Every senior, junior, sophomore, freshman—and all their parents.

I guess nobody outgrows romance.

More adults than teens played.

More husbands than boyfriends bought roses.

People walked so carefully around the squares, as if afraid of destroying romance with a misplaced step. They moaned when they hit Broken Hearts and cheered when they had dates.

I did this, I thought.

"There you are," said Will. "Come on over to Happily Ever After and I'll buy you a soda."

We circled a fifty-foot heart and shared the soda.

And whether it was Happily Ever After, I wouldn't know for years and years. But I was in love with Will and he was in love with me and the game of romance went on.

ABOUT THE AUTHOR

Caroline B. Cooney is the author of many books for young people, including *Family Reunion*; *Goddess of Yesterday*; *The Ransom of Mercy Carter*; *Tune In Anytime*; *Burning Up*; *The Face on the Milk Carton* and its companions, *Whatever Happened to Janie?*, *The Voice on the Radio* and *What Janie Found*; *What Child Is This?*; *Driver's Ed*; *Among Friends*; *Twenty Pageants Later*; and the Time Travel Quartet: *Both Sides of Time*, *Out of Time*, *Prisoner of Time* and *For All Time*.

Caroline B. Cooney lives in Westbrook, Connecticut.